First edition published October 2022

Oftwominds.com
P.O. Box 10847
Hilo HI 96721

Cover: Theresa Barzyk

The Asian Heroine Who Seduced Me

Charles Hugh Smith

With gratitude to my readers.

Section One

Most things fail. When we consider the many potential causes of failure, this shouldn't surprise us. It's too risky, too daunting, or we can't muster the perseverance required. We may misread the situation, or cling to what once worked but no longer works. Or we counted on getting lucky right when our luck ran out. I could lengthen this list, but I'm tired so I'll get to my point: this story is a failure.

It's frowned upon to confess failure at the very start, but this story is already a failure. I probably won't be able to finish it, as this creaking old boat may well split open in the next roller and the ink on these pages will bleed away into the cold Pacific, the journal turned to flotsam along with the boat's three occupants.

I'm no good at telling a story.

There are two ways to tell a story. One is sawing away the untidy bits so there's a beginning, middle and end: *a man was born, he lived, he died*.

The second is to string together different points of view and storylines, presumably to better reflect *real life*.

That's beyond me, so this is *a man was born, he lived and hopefully doesn't die real soon* story.

I'm going to break a rule and start in the now rather than at the beginning. I'm wedged in the bowels of this complaining old yacht which I call The Little Lady, as she has fine lines and is modest in size: *I'm too old and tired for this*, I hear her say. *I should be slipping quietly through the calm waters of a protected bay, enjoying my old age. Instead, these fools sail me straight into the great waves and slashing winds of a typhoon.*

The stench in this closed cabin probably deserves a few words, a retch-producing brew of bilge oil, seawater-diluted vomit, and rancid remains of canned stew. Connoisseurs might detect hints of spilled rum.

A young woman is curled up motionless on one of the built-in cots, drained by seasickness. Let's just say she doesn't look her best. Her long hair is tied up, but I remember her glossy black tresses falling effortlessly down to the small of her back. I also remember her when she looked her best and time stood still.

She says she's pregnant, and I have no reason to doubt her.

The third occupant is slouched against the curved hull on the other side of the cabin, one foot braced against an age-stained teak grating. His eyelids flicker open, and he gazes at me with a detached amusement, as if he senses I'm writing about him. He is annoyingly calm about our decaying chances for a long life, and I can't tell if he's accustomed to cheating Death, or supremely confident by way of mental trickery—*it is my destiny to survive*--or practicing a very high art of detachment he learned while enslaved on a pirate ship plying the Straits of Molucca.

He's lean, another annoying trait, given his enormous appetite when decent food is available. He's a fellow cockroach who's been stepped on with great force. He claims to have escaped a Southeast Asian prison, and I have no reason to doubt him. He doesn't look like much, slim, unkempt tousle of sun-bleached hair, but as the cliché has it, *looks can be deceiving*.

I had to stop writing for a moment, as the poor old gal wallowed in the trough of waves the size of hills and then rose to the crest and pitched down the backside.

Sometimes it's the blend-in women who are the most compelling, and the blend-in men who are the natural survivors. At this delicate point where worm-weakened planks giving way would guarantee the destruction of everything—our lives and the secrets the young woman is duty-bound to preserve and make public—I am willing to place my faith in The Pirate's idiot's-grin confidence.

The Pirate—our private nickname for him—had ably rigged a sea anchor, and so his self-confidence did not seem entirely delusional. A miser with his history and conversation, on rare occasions he'd splurge and sketch one his experiences. But I couldn't tell if these tidbits were a self-serving portrait or if they were offers of a limited-trust friendship.

We were, after all, strangers to each other, sharing cramped fetid quarters, and human nature favors some gestures of friendliness once the pecking order was clear. This was his boat, whether stolen or purchased didn't matter, and he was the Sailor of the Seas, the only one who could get us across the Pacific. Not only that, he'd agreed to our plea despite the many obvious dangers.

I don't know if he is brave, foolhardy, or a contrarian who grabs hold of stupid risks simply because everyone else runs away from them. Maybe he's challenging his destiny to prove itself. Surviving everyday life proves very little, but tumbling off the edge of comfort and convenience—that will establish the boundaries of destiny very quickly.

I am not brave. I had a far easier voyage in mind, and did not anticipate either the official frenzy to catch us on shore or a Pacific typhoon in an old yacht. I fear that first cold gulp of salty passage to the Other Side. I want us to live, to cheat failure, but here in the dim glow of the cabin's battery-powered bulb, so small it reminds me of a flickering Christmas tree light, my mind returns to this: most things fail.

I lack the disposition for real faith, and so my prayers ring hollower than I would like. Like everyone else facing poor odds, I'm anxious to cut a deal with God. It's always an absurdly asymmetric negotiation: we have nothing to offer but promises to become worthy if we survive. *I will make it up to you, if only I get one more chance.* We're like the worst sort of gambler, begging to borrow one more heavy gold coin to put on the next turn of the wheel; we're sure to win this time, we feel it in our palpitating hearts.

In other words, we know we're no worthier than anyone else, but we're touchingly sincere about becoming worthy in our hour of need.

But the young woman is different. She is worthy. And even though she will never admit it, she needs me, even if she doesn't want to, and we need The Pirate, even if we don't want to, and he seems to need us, at least temporarily, even if he doesn't want to.

I'm not sure how much more of this I can take, I hear our creaking boat sigh as we pitch over another peak in the endless howling rollercoaster. *I can't, but I must.* At least this is what I hope.

Even a landlubber like me recognized the yacht's fine lines and the care devoted to its teak woodwork. Given the chance, the interior would scrub up to enough of its former glory to whisper of weekends lazing off Catalina. Its best days are behind it, but it has a history, one we recognize as a form of magic, like a well-loved violin, worn by decades of musicmaking.

Except for a few years in Snow Country, I've always lived within a few kilometers of the Pacific. The restless sea has been formative in ways I can't even identify.

We like to personalize Nature, as if the sea shares some commonality with us. People who drown in the Pacific—and I have almost drowned in the Pacific, pinned to the sand by a breaker—are not victims of a malevolent spirit; we're like plankton or a slimy thread of algae. The Pacific doesn't notice us, much less care about us.

I don't want to drown in the Pacific; I wish the water were warmer, and we were closer to land—a stupid thought, and one I probably shouldn't even put down here—but it is at least a familiar thing, fighting to the surface, chilled to the bone, surprised yet again by the saltiness of the water.

We could have surrendered to the authorities, of course, but she wouldn't choose suicide and neither would I. Given her history, and the three high officials accidentally sent to the Other Side, I didn't need to be persuaded to gamble on escape.

As for the Pirate, I reckon his experience with authority clarified the futility of escape on land, and perhaps the proximity of officialdom's bloodhounds had kindled his sympathy, a fellow fox lending a hand.

This is pure speculation; from what little I know of him—assuming what little he's recounted is true—I think it likely that anyone escaping from a hellhole prison would sympathize with those about to be captured and sent to a hellhole prison.

I'm tired. Tired of the corkscrewing pitches of the boat, tired of being unable to sleep, to really sleep, tired of getting it wrong, tired of my vain hopes for storybook happiness, tired of the nausea, tired of the cramped cabin, tired of being helpless, tired of hoping it will be like when we met, tired of the Pirate's dismissive grin: *this is nothing, you should have been there off Molucca.*

I'm tired of not understanding her and wishing I did, tired of wanting to live long enough to smell land again in the darkness before dawn, to see the creamy line of a breakwater at first light, to steer this once-glorious boat into calm waters and tie up at the first pier, never mind if we have permission, and stagger from the dock to solid ground, lay down on the earth and feel the immense deliciousness that it isn't moving.

But we're far from solid ground and I need to get on with the story. I'm not sure where it should begin, but what I remember is my friend Coltrane gazing up from his black-and-white photos of our street rallies and commenting, "There she is again."

*   *   *

The danger in writing is the untidy bits get left out because we want to save the snapshot where our eyes aren't closed. We want it to be hero's journey, showing off our nice white teeth, like a movie script.

There aren't that many script recipes: *a stranger comes to town, a forbidden love*, and *a quest that ends in a victory against all odds.* Oh, and *all you need is a girl and a gun.* All four fit, so I'm at a loss to pick one.

I don't have a story, really. What I have is a desire to *explain what happened*.

A stranger comes to town. That's her in America, and then me in her Home Country.

A forbidden love. A meeting, an irresistible but necessarily secret courtship, and then forces intervene.

A quest that ends in a victory against all odds. We're still working on that one.

A girl and a gun. Well, yes.

It is old-fashioned to rely on still photos rather than video to capture an event, but I've always been drawn to the way a still photo freezes an instant and allows us to study it with a kind of attention we can't apply to video. It's even more old-fashioned to prefer black-and-white images. Stripping away the color reduces the photo to its essence.

My photographer friend Coltrane who volunteered to document our rallies was intrigued by my request. His approach changed once he saw the black-and-white stills, or rather, his understanding of photography changed.

The rallies are modest events. I'm asked why we bother with gatherings of a few people when online videos garner thousands of views. The physicality is jarring, and I like that. Most people instinctively change their route to avoid any unpleasant entanglement—being hectored for donations, awkward interactions with fanatics, or getting swept up in some dragnet of undesirables.

The authorities' Watchers always position themselves at the edge, close to where passersby increase their pace or pause out of curiosity. When we stage live music, the ratio of the curious to increase-their-pace favors the curious. The Watchers don't try to camouflage their identity. Perhaps they want us to know we're being observed, or disguise isn't worth the effort. Their body language gives them away, and they must know that.

Infiltrators are also easy to spot. They dress up to look credibly marginal, but their enthusiasm for violence gives them away. They stop coming to meetings. Where they're reassigned is a mystery.

The street population is generally listless, though ranters welcome us as a target. As for the activists, let's just say the spectrum of human variety is well-represented. The old people who emerge to reminisce about past glories are especially evocative. Long-dead heroes and heroines are restored to life and the role of the old activist is recounted with modesty or bombast. *We started out like this, too, just a handful of us.*

For some, the thrill of finally finding an audience is inexhaustible. They become agitated when the unwilling audience attempts to politely disengage, and their stridency wearies even the sympathetic.

The idealistic are their own subspecies. I am an idealist, too, of course, but I fancy myself a realist. When someone suggests hanging a bedsheet with a slogan on some imposing structure of oppression, I politely point out that even a king-sized sheet will appear as a postage stamp, what the university students aching to disrupt the bourgeoise in Paris discovered when they unfurled their banner emblazoned with the single word *merde* on the Eiffel Tower.

When somewhat more grizzled idealists—inevitably protected by tenure, a union contract or a spouse toiling away in the bowels of the beast—start talking about the workers taking over the houses in the hills from their undeserving occupants, there is nothing to say, for this variety of revolutionary wilts from any actual work. Strained from patting themselves on the back, they move on to more revolutionary pastures where virtuous cud-chewing is the favored pastime.

In other words, the rallies are failures. Nobody else stages rallies, and so they don't experience the magic of their physicality. It's like an altar imbued with the prayers of generations of worshipers. If you don't kneel on the worn stone, you won't experience the grace that's accumulated like a slow drip of water into a deep pool.

My idealism has one focus: how we create and distribute money. If we don't change the way we create and distribute money, we change nothing. Everything else is just noise. Reforms don't change how money is created and distributed, so the results don't change. This is why homelessness, piles of trash, inequality and despair are everywhere. Reformers pat themselves on the back but the system grinds on unchanged.

Understood as a system, giving banks the privilege of creating money has only one possible result: the wealthiest few benefit at the expense of the many. Inequality is the only possible output.

In the alternative system, money can only be created by human labor: those who perform useful work are paid with the newly created money. Rather than the wealthy having the power to create as much money as they want to buy up the world's assets, the wealthy would have to borrow from those who performed useful work.

This system is called the *Community Labor Integrated Money Economy* because the mechanism for creating money is embedded in the community and labor, not the banks.

I'm told such a system couldn't possibly work. It would work, but those benefiting from the current system have a vested interest in declaring it unworkable.

This is all so blindingly obvious that someday everyone will wonder how humanity could have been so recklessly stubborn, and the shabby mendicants who were dismissed will be recognized as the founders of a radically beneficial enlightenment.

Once you understand this, there's no path back. There is only the path forward.

The data slipped out of her Home Country reveal the workings of money creation and inequality. The frenzy to find us needs no further explanation.

This is my prayer: that we survive not because we are deserving but because we must survive to serve this greater purpose.

In scanning Coltrane's photos of recent rallies, I was looking for shots in which my eyes were closed. My vanity kept me from noticing what he'd noticed: a slim young woman in sunglasses and a hat was almost always in the audience.

Sometimes she wore blue jeans, a faded plaid work shirt and a beret; other times, a sleeveless sundress and a floppy woven hat, or a long tight-waisted dress and a smart fedora.

She stayed away from Watchers and hecklers, and moved about the curious, often using others as screens. On a few occasions, she was in the foreground. Given her sunglasses and hat, her face was never fully visible. She had long dark hair, usually knotted in a chignon but occasionally loose, nearly reaching the small of her back. She appeared older than a university student but not by much. Her posture was erect. She didn't slouch.

Coltrane commented that given her reliable attendance, she was probably a higher-level Watcher. That was certainly plausible. Who else would avoid the Watchers but another watcher? Who else would alternate her appearance between tourist, student, intern and corporate supervisor?

That the local authorities had to make sure nothing got out of hand was understood. But who else had an interest in sparsely attended rallies? It made no sense unless something about us had drawn the attention of someone in a position to assign their own watcher. Isn't it obvious that we're harmless idealists?

Anyone with the slightest interest in surveillance knows that electronic eavesdropping is easier than sending watchers. Was this woman's habitual attendance a subtle signal? If so, what, and to whom?

It was a mystery because we weren't important enough to watch. We assumed our communications were being monitored and we didn't bother with security because everything we said and did was transparent. There was nothing to hide.

One night in the week between rallies I had a strange dream about the mystery woman. In the dream, we met as friends, but I remembered times in bed with her even as we posed as merely friendly. In the dream, I was surprised that we were already lovers, for she was casual with me, as if we'd only ever been friends. It was strange, recalling being lovers even though she did not acknowledge it.

At the next rally, I looked for her in the audience but didn't spot her. To my surprise, I felt a keen disappointment that our mystery woman hadn't come. But I was wrong.

As I was stowing the microphone and speaker in our van, Coltrane interrupted me. "She asked me to photograph her," she exclaimed. "The mystery woman."

Startled by her approach, he naturally agreed to her request. She'd removed her sunglasses and hat, and stood so City Hall was the backdrop. Coltrane showed me the photos and I saw her face for the first time. She was attractive, not beautiful, and her smile was sincere but pensive. Her hair was tied in a ponytail and she wore a fetching sunflower-yellow sundress.

She'd given him two slips of paper, one with her email so he could send her the photos, and a sealed one for me. I glanced at the hand-written note and by instinct pocketed it before he could read it. "It just says she admires my work, blah-de-blah," I told him.

The note was more interesting than I let on.

"Would you be so kind as to meet me at The Black Cat tonight at 9? Please ask for Christine C."

If she was from Asia, she'd probably chosen a Western name to ease communication. The note sounded like a non-native speaker, but this was just a guess.

The awkward formal tone of her note was at odds with the sketchy nature of The Black Cat, an invitation-only club reputedly favored by the criminal element. It was the last place I would expect a fresh-faced young Asian woman would pick for a first date—and that's if she could get an invitation.

Her block letters were equally noteworthy, as each letter was more cursive than angular.

The meeting mixed anticipation and trepidation. Naturally I wanted to appear to be everything I'm not: good-looking, charming, erudite, impressive--but would settle for not looking like a fool. I was intensely curious how she would explain her interest in our lackluster rallies.

The venue was equally mixed. To experience such a mysterious club was definitely a draw, but being out of my depth was also on my mind. Fear is good in healthy doses. So is being ready to react.

My only paying job was night watchman for an eccentric property owner who'd inherited a marginal used-book store and the building that housed it. The bookstore remained marginal but the building was well-sited and valuable. I think he hired us not because he needed security but because he wanted to support what we were doing in our daytime lives.

My fellow watchman was a veteran, an interesting fellow for multiple reasons. His way of staying awake was martial arts training, which required my participation. He enjoyed teaching me by beating me in no-contact sparring, where he'd explain each move after he'd demonstrated it on me. Clearing away boxes of old encyclopedias, we set up a heavy punching bag in the basement and kept ourselves awake until we split sleeping shifts.

On our rounds we carried a length of stout bamboo—better than a knife or firearm, my partner said, and after a few months of training, I could see why. You can't undo pulling the trigger, he explained, and a knife or gun can be used against you. The bamboo length extended your range and was very quick and hard to defend against.

Was I a match for a trained fighter? Of course not. But I wasn't going to stand there and get punched in the face, either.

The watchman job was minimum pay, and so I shared a group house and kept minimal belongings and expenses. My wardrobe offered few choices. I decided on black jeans and a dark-gray designer-labeled jacket I'd picked up at a jumble sale. It had a few small moth holes but was presentable in a dark nightclub.

Wishful thinking is human nature, and I am not immune. I told myself to enjoy this meeting for what it is, a novelty. I fancy myself a realist. I'm not dangerous enough or successful enough to be attractive to women, and not willing to suffer the grinding wheel of online romance. In other words, I was alone.

My fellow watchman grumbled at my request to find a replacement, but the truth was it was not a job requiring two people other than to provide company.

The Black Cat entrance was down a dimly lit alley off Sleazy Sixth. Denizens of the district clustered at the entrance to accost passersby as they hurried their pace. The employee at the entrance was not oversized, but he looked capable. His suit looked good on him.

He sized me up. "I'm here at the invitation of Christine C.," I said. A hint of skepticism enlivened his impassive gaze, and he said, "Wait here."

A resident of the area shuffled past and mumbled, "Good evening, Officer," to my amusement. Did I really look like Vice Squad?

The trim bouncer emerged from the subdued interior and said, "Follow me, sir."

The "sir" was instructive.

The club combined the scents and sensibility of a Chinese restaurant with a wayward artist's touch and someone's notion of a British club: the front of the space was dark paneled walls and leather chairs, fronting a small stage where a suitably hirsute musician put his upright bass through its paces and a female guitarist with pink-tinged blond locks fiddled with the tone controls of her sunburst hollow-body electric guitar.

A large plaster sculpture of a female breast, a good meter high, took pride of place beside the stage. Strings of red paper lanterns adorned the space above the sculpture and the stage. A few inflated blowfish dangled above an aquarium on the other side of the stage.

The sculpture's prominent nipple looked well-worn from human caresses.

A coatroom and discreet bar occupied the corner opposite the stage. A waiter in a classic white jacket served the guests in the chairs. The chocolate-skinned female bartender was similarly uniformed.

A hidden kitchen served the premises, as hot oil and Ma-Po tofu scented the air.

The leather chairs were grouped to enable conversations. The chairs' occupants were mostly middle-aged men and women with an air of comfortably prosperous influence. If a criminal element was present, it was of the collusion type in which understandings were reached without being recorded.

Maybe the reputation and the seedy location were covers for more genteel forms of larceny, or maybe they gave the members an enjoyable sensation of slumming.

The bouncer led me through this lounge area to a space lined with large booths a step above the floor, each made private with red velvet curtains. Muted laughter and conversations were audible; it didn't take much to imagine various intimacies in the quiet booths.

Despite my pep talk about enjoying the novelty, my heartrate increased when the bouncer pulled the curtain aside and ushered me into a Japanese-style space with tatami mats, a low table and zabuton cushions for seating. Christine C. arose to greet me, and her smile was welcoming and free of the nervousness I felt.

She was not model-beautiful or beautifully made up, but beautiful for reasons that are more challenging to describe, the sort enhanced by what might otherwise be modest flaws: freckled cheeks, her mouth a bit too wide, slight dimples when she smiled. Her sun-burnished skin was smooth and healthy, her eyebrows were straight and fine, and her teak-colored eyes intelligent and quick. There's an attractiveness unique to mixed blood and she had it, perhaps a quarter of this and the rest of that.

For our first meeting she'd chosen to wear a plain black halter blouse that showed her figure and bare shoulders to good effect and a peasant-style skirt of multi-colored, mixed-texture fabrics. Her dark cascade of hair was pinned up in a chignon, revealing her graceful neck. Her smile revealed even white teeth. She had the glow of the well-off and an unself-conscious confidence. She was poised, slightly shy and visibly curious about me.

In other words, she was stunning.

And needless to say, out of my league.

"Thank you for accepting my invitation," she said as we shook hands. My hand looked huge and rough compared to hers. Her accent was the BBC-tinged standard of former British colonies and of private schools on the English model. Her voice was even and warm, like a note on the low string of a violin.

"It was a great surprise," I replied. Following her lead, I sat down, grateful for the flexibility won by my evenings of martial arts. She smiled and said, "I owe you an explanation. I'm here for a program at the university, and my parents have forbidden me from dating. They're afraid I might meet an American and not return home."

This clicked with her behavior at the rallies, and I asked, "You mean you're followed?"

The answer embarrassed her. "Yes."

"Do they monitor your email and phone?"

She nodded affirmatively. That explained the hand-written note. I said, "Your parents know you're attractive and are understandably fearful."

"Needlessly," she said, and her expression was hard to read.

"How did you choose this place, and get here undetected?"

Tilting her head playfully, she replied, "Girls have secrets."

"Is why you're at our rallies a secret, too?"

"That's why you're here," she said. "I'm interested in you and your work."

Surprised by this open admission, I said, "I'm honored, but you've seen the low attendance. Nobody's interested in our work."

"Then why do you do it?"

"Because it's important."

"Even if nobody cares?"

"Especially if nobody cares."

Her eyes widened and she gave me a dimpled smile. "Many people are idealistic until money is involved."

"I'm safe from temptation, as there's no money involved."

She opened her black clasp purse and removed a cashier's check drawn on a Swiss bank. The sum was about five times my annual income. The check was made out to me.

Who offers you this much money other than someone who has multiples of this amount? And who offers it in a first meeting? People offering large sums of money right off the bat have something other than your best interests in mind.

"It's not fake," she assured me. "You can deposit this tomorrow and see it's real."

I glanced at the check and had to smile. "And what's this for?"

"Suppose it was for giving up your work on inequality."

My incredulity must have been obvious. "Are we really this much of a threat?"

She shook her head. "It's not for your group, it's for you. Just you."

What was she getting out of this? Was this this some sort of grand Dickensian gesture of alms to the poor, in which I touch my cap and promise eternal gratitude to my better?

My smile broadened. "Oh, I see. A test of my idealism." I slid the check back to her. "I'm not trying to be saint. I don't really have any use for this much money."

Nonplussed, she said, "Of course you do. Who wouldn't like a nice car, a vacation, maybe even a house?"

"More trouble than they're worth," I replied, and I was sincere. There was a time when I would have snatched the money with greedy gratitude, but now the burdens of possessions weighed heavily.

"This money is yours to spend, no strings attached."

The game was unexpected, and its purpose remained a mystery. "Some people don't believe in luck or coincidence. I don't believe in no strings attached money."

The white-jacketed waiter coughed to announce his presence and slid the curtain aside to deliver two glistening flutes of champagne. "Miss Christine, your champagne." As I took the proffered flutes, Christine thanked him as she slipped him a neatly folded bill, and he discreetly closed the curtain.

Whoever she was, Miss Christine had the respect of the staff.

I handed her one of the flutes, and our fingers touched. Neither of us moved, and something akin to an electrical current passed between us. "To Miss Christine's health," I said, raising my glass. "To no strings attached," she replied, and we each sipped the champagne. It was dry but not too dry. In other words, expensive.

"Let's say we only meet this once," she said. "Once you don't have to impress me with your idealism, wouldn't you take the money? Isn't it like finding a blank check on the sidewalk?"

Her urgency impressed me. Why was my refusal so unacceptable?

"All money has strings," I said. "I really don't want those attachments."

"Then you could spend it on your group," she insisted. "Buy better equipment, do more promotion."

I shook my head. "That's not how it works. The more you have, the less you do. The less you have, the more you do. Having all this money would destroy the group, not help it."

Her skepticism remained firm and I said, "Let's say this is all the money you have in the world, everything but next month's rent and food. Would you still offer it to me?"

Her eyes widened at this reversal and she had no response.

"You assume I'm a phony and as greedy as the next guy," I told her. "Fair enough. That describes most do-gooders. But I don't stand on a rock declaring my sainthood. I'd love success as much as anyone, but money isn't the success I want. It's a distraction."

Pouting, she said, "You may regret your pride later."

"You think that I'm not actually idealistic, I'm just prideful of looking idealistic."

She nodded. "It's possible, isn't it?"

"That could be," I acknowledged. "There's no way to prove idealism. Any gesture looks like pride."

She considered this, and I added, "If I tear up this check, you'd call it pride. If you want me to keep it in the hopes that I'll cash it and prove you're right, I'm a phony. If you think I'm just a phony Saint Francis, fine, I gain nothing by changing your mind. I didn't seek you out or ask for your approval."

I drained the champagne and said, "Thank you for the champagne and invitation."

She looked hurt and I said, "You're prideful, too, of your cynicism. You think everyone who isn't greedy and cynical is phony, but cynics are the ultimate phonies."

That stung, and her eyes flashed hot. I thought of a few more hurtful things to say but reckoned I'd done enough damage. After all, I could be a phony, someone good at being impassioned in public and greedy in private. So many were. I would probably think I was a phony, too.

Recovering, she said, "You don't like being challenged."

"What do the real phonies do? Protest the loudest and then have a good laugh in private after they've cashed the check?"

"Yes, they have a good laugh in private after they take the money," she said.

"And what would a saint do? Laugh the whole thing off? Do you know any saints we could put to the test? Give them this check and have them sleep with horny virgins?"

She didn't respond and I wanted to add, *I guess you only know phonies*, but that wasn't fair. I had no idea who she knew.

"I don't know any saints, either," I said. "I'm sorry, the whole topic is tiresome."

She looked worn as well. It was a poor showing by both of us.

Lifting her champagne glass, she poured half in my glass, as if her instinct was to share rather than waste.

Her gesture changed me, and I said, "I didn't mean to offend you. It was very kind of you to offer me a small fortune, no strings attached."

Sliding the check toward me, she said, "Would you please accept it as a gift? Maybe someday it will become useful, and you'll be glad you accepted it."

Put in terms of a gift and potential utility at a later date, I decided to accept. "Okay, I'll hold it uncashed." Folding the check, I placed it in my jacket pocket and raising my half-full champagne flute, I said, "A toast to your generous gift and the spirit behind it."

Her smile was wan, but she raised her glass and took a sip.

The faint sound of the upright bass seeped through the curtains, and we gazed awkwardly at one another.

"I've seen some of your life," she ventured. "Would you like to see some of mine?"

"Of course," I said, and I hoped she sensed my sincerity.

To lighten the conversation, I affected a conspiratorial tone. "Do you trust me with your secret?"

She replied in kind. "I already have."

Draining her glass, she asked, "If I take you home, will you give me cooties?"

I laughed, and so did she.

"No, I'm perfectly healthy."

"A girl can kiss you and not worry?"

She continued to surprise me. "Yes. But no girl has been that bold in a long time."

"Too bad I'm not bold," she replied, and though we'd just met, it was an inside joke. Everything she'd crammed into our short time together had been bold.

"What about you?" I asked. "Do I have anything to worry about?"

Lowering her voice, she said, "We can joke about it, but we can't be seen together, not even once. It would be bad for me."

I nodded, and she continued. "You must follow these instructions exactly. Can I trust you?"

"Yes."

"I've watched you, but you know nothing about me. Can you trust me anyway?"

Her urgency struck me anew, and it gave me pause. It seemed like an elaborate game, fooling the paranoid parents' watchers by sneaking behind the hedge to make out. But her anxiety was not playacting.

Retrieving her purse, she handed me a note and a folded black felt cap. "There's a guy who lives in my building who's tall like you and wears a cap like this. Sometimes he hums a song under his breath, *the rain in Spain stays mainly on the plain*, things like that. He takes the stairs two at a time. Can you mimic that?"

"Yes."

"Walk through the laundromat and go out the back door. There's a wooden staircase. Go to the third floor and use this key to open the hallway door, and this one to open the first apartment on the right."

She handed me two keys and then added, "If you see the guy in the cap, take yours off and walk with a limp. If anyone else is in the hall, keep walking and take the stairs at the end to the second floor. Make sure you're not seen."

"You're good at this," I said. "Have you had a lot of practice?"

She picked up the implication. "No, you're the first."

"Even at The Black Cat?"

She nodded assent. No wonder the bouncer's initial impression of me improved: Miss Christine's first male visitor.

She slid the note across to me and I saw it was an artfully sketched map. There were no street names to reveal the location. She put her finger on a large rectangle. "Here's The Black Cat." Moving her finger a few inches, she said, "I live close by."

"Do we leave a few minutes apart?"

"No," she replied. "I'll leave by another exit." Before I could ask any more questions, she said, "Wait five minutes. When you leave, tip the doorman." She handed me a week's rent in folded bills.

"Is he really that good?"

She smiled coyly. "Why? Are you tempted to keep this and give him a dollar?"

"Very tempted," I replied. "Could you get me a job here? I'd look good in a white jacket."

She snapped her purse closed and said, "Don't be late. You'll make me worried."

* * *

After exiting the alley, I considered practicing walking with a limp but felt foolish. Fortunately, I didn't see the Humming Man in the Black Cap when I stepped out of the laundromat and ascended the stairs two at a time, laboring to hum *Summertime*.

Pausing to catch my breath, I readied myself for more surprises and opened the midnight-blue apartment door. The interior was dark except for a single low light illuminating a corner of the living room floor. Befitting the age of the wooden building, the apartment was modest: a small living room, cramped dining nook, kitchen, bath and a closed door to the bedroom. The opaque curtains let in no light but moved slightly, indicating partially open windows. A large poster of an

Asian female's made-up eyes gazed down on the living room's bare wood floor and neat stack of red zabuton cushions. The scent of sesame oil and chilis perfumed the air.

Christine emerged from the kitchen in a red and white striped apron. She still wore her black halter-top blouse but the multi-colored skirt had been shed. "I'm making *Ants Climbing a Tree*. Would you like some?"

The dish demanded tedious preparation. Carrots had to be diced, scallions sliced, the glass noodles soaked, the ground meat seasoned and the sauce prepared. She'd done all this long before our rendezvous at The Black Cat.

Following her into the narrow kitchen, I watched her turn the noodles into the sizzling wok and quickly stir in the seasoning sauce as the fried chilis stung our eyes. Sliding the mixture into a waiting bowl, she delivered it to the small table, apologizing, "It's a simple dinner, just one dish." From the rusting refrigerator she pulled a chilled bottle of Chenin Blanc and handed it to me to open while she served the glass noodles in shallow bowls decorated with lotus flowers. As she removed her apron, I saw that she'd exchanged her skirt for black shorts.

Averting my gaze from her legs with difficulty, I poured us each a half-glass of wine, saying, "There's nothing simple about this dish."

We clinked glasses in a silent toast and the kitchen light flickered. Arising, she brought a candle in a cast aluminum holder and lit it. "The electricity here comes and goes," she said.

"You could afford newer rooms."

"I can do what I want here. Nobody minds if I paint the walls."

Her version of the classic dish was a revelation. "The chili peppers are a perfect balance," exclaimed.

"You know how to cook?"

"We share meal prep in the house," I explained. "My housemates are much better cooks than I am. I've learned from them."

She gave me an expectant grin. "And what can you make for me?"

"It's not three Michelin stars," I replied. "They like my Vietnamese grilled chicken, my *Pommes de Terre Lyonnaise* is okay, my Sambar is passable, my tomatillo *Enchiladas Verde* are not bad..."

"Why hasn't some woman claimed you just to have you in the kitchen?"

"If they only got the cooking, maybe," I said. "But they have to listen to me, and that's boring."

"Maybe you talk too much."

"Undoubtedly," I replied.

"Maybe you don't have enough fun."

"Isn't changing the world fun?"

"What's that saying about changing yourself rather than trying to change the world?"

I raised my glass to her. "My sanctimonious balloon has been popped. I get that, but is it really one or the other?"

"I don't know," she replied.

"Me, neither," I confided. "I find myself dreaming of slipping away."

"What would you do with yourself?"

"Grow sweet potatoes, keep quiet and cook for a woman."

She laughed and I asked, "What about you? Why haven't your parents approved Mr. Right?"

Toying with her glass, she said, "It's not that easy."

Rather than press her, I awaited her next topic but the verve she displayed at the club had softened. At first, I reckoned her preoccupied, but concluded that she wanted to say something but thought better of it.

Clearing the dishes, she announced, "There's dessert. But not just yet."

As she washed the few dishes, I put away the leftover wine and noodles. Standing in the hallway between the kitchen and bath, I glanced back at the front door and noticed a violin case propped in the corner.

"Do you play, or is that violin for decoration?"

"I play a little, not very well," she replied. "My parents insisted."

"Would you do me the honor of playing for me?"

"I'm rusty," she said dismissively.

"It's just for fun between friends," I replied.

She gave me a wry look. "Have I been promoted from cynic to friend?"

"Friends share meals, don't they?"

She hesitated and I said, "I'm not a critic. I play guitar, embarrassingly badly. It would be fun to hear you play, even *Twinkle, Twinkle, Little Star*."

Her smile brought forth her dimples and she said, "I guess I can do a little better than that."

I followed her into the living room and took a cushion while she opened the case and began tuning the violin. She knew what she was doing, as the strings were already in tune.

"Cover your eyes," she instructed. "You're making me nervous."

Leaning back against the wall crossed-legged, I put my hand over my eyes. The slit between my second and third fingers allowed me a partial view of her. Her posture was erect as always, and she played a few scales and then opening of *Fur Elise*. After a pause, she began playing Beethoven's Romance Number Two, a piece I recognized from my years with my first lover. Watching her play felt like cheating, and so I lowered my head and just listened to the sweetness of the melody, rendered with warmth and vibrancy. She played not just well, but with verve and tenderness.

Playing from memory, she stopped partway through, and paused again. Reckoning that was the end of her performance, I raised my head and opened my eyes. Facing the wall, she seemed lost in thought and unaware of my presence.

Without any preparation she launched into a cadenza that quickly reached a ferocity unlike any I'd ever heard. Long bow pulls that seemed intended to break the string, jagged arpeggios, silvery atonal riffs, hammer notes, furious repetitions of melodies, fluid shifts from major to minor key, and crescendos building and collapsing. It wasn't technical brilliance, or showing off technique; it was an outpouring of intensity that changed me.

You may think that's an extravagant claim, that what I mean is her playing *moved me*. But it's not just revelations or experiences that change us. Witnessing *what is possible* changes us, too.

Her intensity drained, she set the instrument down and closed the case. It felt as if she too had been left breathless by the outburst. It expressed something that had been welling up and then dammed up.

Maybe there were no words to express it, and so her violin became her voice.

I wanted to ask if that was entirely improvised or based on an incredible cadenza, but rather than risk ruining the moment, I waited.

Offering her hand to help me up, she said, "Don't get any ideas, but I want to show you my bedroom."

She pushed open the door and I saw what she meant about her freedom to repaint the walls. The heavy curtains were black, the walls were black, the bed frame was black, the shiny comforter was black and the dresser was black. A silver candelabra on the dresser was the only decoration other than a large decoupage of gold and silver leaf pieces in a silver frame depicting an elaborate kimono.

"Excuse me," she said, and went to the bathroom. I marveled at her cinematic décor and her apparently endless ability to surprise me.

The overhead light went out and she emerged from the bathroom to retrieve a box of matches. Her match flared up, scenting the air with sulfur, and she lit a single candle in the candelabra.

She came to me and our eyes met. "I told you the power is unreliable."

"Fortunately, you're prepared," I replied.

The candlelight bathed her mischievous expression in a warm glow.

Pulling her glossy black mane aside so it fell down her back, she said, "If you want, you can kiss me."

Her halter bowknot must have come loose, for after she swept her hair aside it suddenly gave way, and her blouse fell to her waist. In the glow of the candle, I wondered if she'd modeled the sculpture in The Black Cat.

As her blouse slid soundlessly to the floor, her shorts also succumbed to gravity. The loose knot giving way cascaded more than her clothing, and I found her bedsheets were dark gray.

Her musical outburst had not drained her of intensity or expression. This too changed me.

The loosened halter succumbing to gravity was more than good fortune, of course. Her clothing slipping to the floor seemingly by happenstance was as well prepared as the *Ants Climbing a Tree*. I was disinclined to complain about either one.

*   *   *

I apologize for the economic analogies, but it captures the dynamics so perfectly I can't resist.

In economic terms, Christine and I both had months or even years of pent-up demand. When the supply increases to meet this sustained surge of demand, it's a Heavenly alignment of the stars.

In a financial analogy, the greater the liquidity, the happier the exchange. Assets increase in value, secure bonds become even more valuable, and the *wealth effect* arises: the more you have, the greater your ability to enjoy even more.

Innovation and stability are both rewarded. Variety and novelty spark demand, but so do tried-and-true comforts.

Sometimes she wanted something specific, other times she let me choose. It was a carefree splurge of demand I'd never experienced, and her soft-eyed permissions persuaded me that she'd never felt such comfort before, either.

I liked her physicality. Not the interchangeable variety, where paper bags could be placed over attractive young women's heads and any of their bodies would do. I mean her scent and how it became more compelling with time; the smell of her hair; the taste of her skin, which I accused her of coating with thinned honey; her needless embarrassment over her nubby toes; the wisps of hair at her temples; her languid lack of fussiness; the way she squeezed my waist when we met each night, revealing her strength, and the way she stayed in bed and wanted me there, rather than leaping up to shower it all away.

And her humor. Drifting amidst the clouds of giddy goofiness, I once joked, "If you weren't on birth control, you might have triplets in eight months."

Shifting onto her side, she gave me a wide-eyed look of wonderment. "Will I sprout a third breast?"

"That would be awkward," I agreed. "But there would be an upside. No more wearing a bra."

We also devised suitably schoolgirl-schoolboy assembly instructions:

1. Inflate the device to full length and firmness.
2. Insert until fully seated and squeeze firmly.
3. Continue until both lubricants are released.
4. Deflate and remove until next use is required.

In other words, we clicked, not just as hungry bodies but as hungry souls.

Secrecy set our routine.

I would enter after she'd turned off the lights and feigned going to sleep around 9 pm.

To avoid too obvious a routine, she had me semi-randomly arrive by a stealthier route. A mere foot separated her building from the one next door at the street entrance, where the adjacent building's fire escape occupied the fifteen feet between the building. This stairway was hidden behind a façade, so that from the sidewalk there was no space between the buildings. By climbing up the fire escape, I could reach a window in the interior stairwell of Christine's building. Christine had removed the window lock, and none of the residents even noticed.

All this seemed outlandishly covert, but she assured me the surveillance was real. "They only show themselves if they want you to know you're being watched, like at your rallies. They use hidden cameras and microphones and hack your mobile phone."

"Aren't you afraid they've bugged your flat?"

"Of course, they've bugged my flat and phone," she replied. "But this isn't my flat. I never bring my phone here. This is a friend's place that she lets me use while she's traveling."

Unable to mask my shock, I blurted, "But this place is so *you*."

"I made it my own. I hope she likes it."

"When will she come back?"

"Don't worry, not for a while," she said. "And you know I have to go home at the end of the program. I can't put it off. Please don't even ask."

"You sneak in here, too?"

"Yes. There's no other way we could have this time together."

"All this just to keep you from dating?"

"That's real, but it's not just that," she explained. "My father is a bigshot in politics and my mother is ill. He has enemies who would enjoy using me to get back at him."

"Having an American boyfriend would be an embarrassment? That sounds so parochial."

"Loyalties matter, face matters," she said wearily. "My life is not my own at home. I can't explain it, it's too complicated. You have to know Asian cultures to understand."

"I'd like to try," I said.

Her voice added frustration to weariness. "We all have duties. I'm an only child. You have your group."

I started to ask another question and she cut me off. "Can't you see that talking about this makes me miserable? Can't you just let me have the last of our carefree time together?"

"Yes."

Her shoulders slumped and she said, "If only you knew how much it means to me to not be worried right now."

"Okay, no worries," I assured her. "I understand more than you imagine."

Looking down, she murmured, "If only that could be true."

Behind our retreat into goofy humor, I understood that she was asking me to mask my own misery to alleviate hers. It was a sacrifice I tried to fulfill.

"Just satisfy one curiosity, if it's not too worrisome," I said. "How did you get to be a member of The Black Cat?"

She smiled with some of her usual mischievousness. "That's easy. I'm a part-owner."

Unable to hide my surprise, I said, "Miss Christine sure has a lot of secrets."

Nudging me, she said, "Isn't that why you love her?"

"Oh, she's irresistible for many reasons." Feigning a sudden revelation, I exclaimed, "I bet you were the model for The Black Cat's boob sculpture. I am so envious of the sculptor, getting to stare at you for hours."

Faux-slapping my shoulder, she said, "Silly. The sculptor was a woman. She didn't need a model."

"But being an art model is tempting, isn't it, if you could do it in secret?"

She didn't reply, and her expression became somber. "Promise me you won't try to follow me. You'd only ruin everything."

Somewhat defensively, I said, "It hadn't even occurred to me."

"But it's tempting, isn't it?"

"If you enter a burning building," I said, "I'm following you in to rescue you."

"Why would I go into a burning building?"

"You wouldn't, but suppose the back burst into flames right after you went in, and you couldn't see the flames."

"Isn't it a bit much to assume little old me would need rescuing? I'll escape just fine all by myself."

What seemed likely to me is the building bursting into flames not by coincidence but *because she entered*.

"We all need to be rescued sometimes, even the strongest, smartest, richest of us."

Her expression brightened into a sly grin. "You're right. When I see you go into a building and it bursts into flames, I'll rescue you."

* * *

A week later she met me in the darkened flat with exciting news. She'd recruited a doppelganger, a young woman of similar height, figure and hair, to pose as her and occupy her apartment. This freed us to spend the day out in the world—our first and perhaps only such opportunity. "Can you borrow a car?" she asked. "Don't use the group van or rent a car. We don't want any transaction records."

Our group had a few wealthy donors, and one restored classic cars as a hobby. He was friendly enough, and I was prepared to beg. "I think I can manage that. Where are we going?"

With the expression of a temptress, she replied, "You'll find out tomorrow."

"What about our disguises?"

"What's the least likely thing you'd wear?"

"A jacket and tie."

"There's your disguise. But make it a bit arty—a loud tie, something like that."

"What about you?"

"You'll see." Her excitement was a window into the restrictions of her life. She deserved liberation.

"Aren't you happy we can spend a day together?" she asked.

"Of course. I'm just caught off-guard, like a miracle occurred."

After our pillow-fight celebration of the news, I called our donor and played the hot-new-romance card, which worked as hoped. He offered me a two-seater classic convertible, canary-yellow, recently tuned, but *Lordy-Lord, be careful, the body took work you wouldn't believe*.

I believed, and was nervous about driving such a costly car, but swallowed my anxiety for the sake of adventure. It was likely my one chance to have a normal daytrip with Christine.

A roommate about my height loaned me a light-gray linen jacket, a flamboyant red paisley tie and a pin-striped Oxford shirt. With black jeans and dark sunglasses, I almost looked presentable.

The weather was warm and clear, and after a quick lesson on driving the convertible from the generous donor—push-button starter, manual gearbox, something I'd mastered on a construction job during university—I drove with excruciating caution to the rendezvous spot we'd decided on last night, the sidewalk fronting the public library.

I didn't recognize her at first. I was looking for an Asian woman of her height in subdued attire when a young woman with big oval sunglasses and a bright blue kerchief wearing a revealing black tube top and a skimpy yellow skirt approached and leaned down to greet me. A fringe of dyed blond hair escaped the kerchief, and Christine laughed at my surprise.

Placing her blue handbag behind the seat, she settled into the low-slung sports car and said, "Fooled you, didn't I?"

Her shoulders, midriff and legs were bared to excellent effect, and gazing at the happy beauty beside me, I pondered the fearful mystery of why someone as talented and attractive as Christine had chosen me. Various theories occurred to me—she was engaged to be married when she returned home and I was the semi-exotic final fling, different enough for zest but not dangerously so—but the care she took to evade surveillance exceeded any pretense. No one would maintain such vigilance for show. Her fear of exposure was real.

Glancing at me, she joked, "One of your roommates has good taste."

She handed me an address and I knew better than to inquire further. The mystery was part of the fun.

Once on the road, we had to shout over the background noise of the engine and wind. "I'm glad you approve. And congratulations on your telepathy. How else could you match your yellow skirt to the yellow car?"

"It's not quite the same yellow."

"I love your bohemian rebel artist look," I shouted. "The blond wig, it's the real you."

She looked pleased and shouted, "Maybe so."

The address was in an old industrial area by the docks that had yet to be gentrified. A scattering of old houses had escaped being torn down for warehouses, and our destination was a brick building which judging by the wheat sheafs at the apex of the façade had once been a commercial bakery. The old bungalow between the brick bakery and an ugly corrugated metal warehouse had been painted bright yellow and green. A gnarled lemon tree wedged against the sidewalk managed to survive in the small square of hardened dirt left to it, and Christine took a camera from her handbag to snap a photo of it. The tree was the only bit of living greenery in sight.

"It looks lonely," she said.

"It's a survivor, like you."

I expected a laugh but her expression was pensive. Plucking one of the lemon that had yet to fall to the barren square of earth, I sliced it open with my pocketknife and handed her half. The scent was fresh and clean, such a contrast with the lifeless gray surroundings. She sucked on the juice with a childlike enthusiasm and then squeezed the half-lemon into her open mouth.

"Try it," she said. "it's good for you."

After I dutifully copied her extraction method, she took the two halves and tossed them playfully into the top leaves of the tree.

Muffled music filtered out of the brick building and we slid open the heavy rusted door.

The interior smelled of fiberglass resin and wet clay. Sliding the door shut as quietly as we could, we stood in the shadows of the vestibule, watching the scene being filmed in the brightly lit rear of the cavernous space.

An enormous, smoothly finished sculpture of a female buttocks glistened in the light, and gaily dressed young women were clambering up behind the rounded masses and sliding down the glossed mounds to mattresses lining the floor. Off to one side, a loudspeaker blared *Take Five* played on sitar and tabla drums. The young frolickers waved their arms, whooped and sought acrobatic poses on their way down the monumental derriere.

The song ended with a flourish and the female director behind the camera shouted "Cut!"

As the winded cast gathered around a refreshment table, I followed Christine to the paint-spattered working area along the side wall, where a matronly woman in a smock was standing. With close-cropped graying hair, she looked out of place amidst such zaniness.

"Marianne, this is my friend Gibson," Christine said. We shook hands, and she examined me as if sizing me for a tailored suit. "She's the sculptor of The Black Cat piece," Christine explained, and Marianne added dryly, "Picasso had his Blue phase, I'm in my tits and ass phase, as you can see."

Christine laughed, and Marianne said, "Actually, The Black Cat tit and this big butt are both commissions."

"For a film?" I asked.

"No, an art student saw it and a friend in film school asked to use it."

"How did you two meet?" I asked as innocently as I could manage.

Before Christine could answer, Marianne said, "Christine managed to send The Black Cat commission my way."

"Did she model for you?"

Glancing at Christine, she said, "It's an idealized breast, no model needed."

"Just tell him," Christine urged.

"No, she didn't model for that piece," Marianne said, "though it's a compliment to both of us that you think so."

As I looked around her workspace tables, clay pieces in progress and metal casting paraphernalia, Marianne explained, "I make light of these pieces, but they're expressions of the fertility goddess. Ancient clay fertility goddess figurines were always well-endowed."

As Christine and Marianne headed for the cast's refreshment table, I wandered about the workspace. Behind a jury-rigged pink fabric screen held in place with wooden clothespins, I found what looked to be a finished or nearly finished clay figure about half a meter in height. I recognized it as a three-dimensional version of the bare-breasted woman in Delacroix's painting *Liberty Leading the People*. The figure was noticeably Asian in stature and features, and the resemblance to Christine was striking. Where Delacroix's Liberty wore a cap, the Asian Liberty's long hair swirled behind her as her raised arm brandished a flag. Marianne's careful phrasing implied Christine might have modeled for another sculpture, and this one of Liberty was too much like Christine to be coincidence.

Their reactions when they found me confirmed my conclusion. Marianne was openly amused while Christine's buoyancy faded. Rather than put either on the spot, I said, "An Asian Liberty. It's glorious."

"It's almost ready," Marianne said, and as Christine guided me away, I whispered to her, "I know it's you."

"You're imagining things," she reprimanded me, but something in her expression suggested being pleased I'd seen through their artful dodge.

The artist and her patron/model embraced and Christine said, "I'm so happy I could visit your studio." This surprised me, as nothing in her behavior reflected a first visit. Or was this staged for my benefit?

As we exited the brick studio, Christine said, "I packed a picnic lunch. Take me somewhere beautiful."

I quickly settled on a coastal park some distance away with a scenic white-sand beach cove and craggy rock promontories surrounded by a scattering of well-heeled vacation homes nestled amidst picturesque pines.

The two-lane highway wound precariously along the coast, offering the classic roadster a chance to stretch its cornering and acceleration on the occasional straightaways.

Though occupied by the challenges of the road, on straight stretches I stole sidelong glances at my companion, marveling anew at her youth, confidential connections, delectable features and exposed shoulders and legs. In her oversized oval shades, tube top, short golden skirt, windswept blue kerchief and fringe of fake blond locks, she was a model for all that was free and fun. And most amazingly, she was with me.

We soon gave up shouting to be heard and she seemed content to slouch in the bucket seat, gazing at the scenery and smiling when she caught me soaking her up with my gaze.

The parking lot was full and the beach crowded with people taking advantage of the light breeze and bright sun. I risked a parking ticket so we could stretch our legs and go barefoot.

Christine had asked me not to take photos of her lest my phone be hacked, but I snuck one photo of her as she leaped off a waist-high bleached-white driftwood log. Since I was behind her, the photo captured only her bent-knee leap in midair and the flutter of her skirt, blue kerchief and blond locks. Since no one could identify her from this photo, I kept it. It was my sole photo of her.

We compared our footprints in the wet sand, splashed about in the cold water of the Pacific washing up on the beach, and watched a small Asian girl happily riding the wavelets lapping onto the beach as if they were mighty surf waves. She wore a purple swimsuit and matching inflatable flotation sleeves, and laughed merrily as each wavelet carried her a few feet and then retreated. Her pleasure did not diminish.

I glanced at Christine, and wondered if the girl reminded her of carefree childhood memories, or a dearth of such memories. Her expression suggested nostalgia.

"It's too crowded here," I said. She agreed and we returned to the roadster, shaking the sand from our feet to minimize the cleanup when I returned to car.

The further we drove from the city, the thinner the crowds, and I pulled over at a viewpoint. It was a brilliantly clear day, warm enough to raise a sheen of sweat on her bare arms once we got out and walked to the stone wall surrounding the lookout.

A small cove was partially visible below the parking area, and I saw a single couple sunbathing on the half-moon of gray sand. "Let's go down there for our picnic," I suggested, and Christine eyed the rough informal trail down the rocky slope with hesitation.

"It looks slippery," she said.

"We'll be careful," I encouraged her. She looked down dubiously, and I slung her bag over my shoulder. I'd noticed the car's owner had left big beach towels, a first-aid kit and jugs of water in the tiny trunk.

Stuffing the towels on top of her bag, I took her hand and said, "You're coming whether you planned to or not. This is our one chance for a little adventure."

Stepping down onto the rock outcropping, I counseled, "Just follow where I put my feet. I'll steady you."

It was a new experience to see her hesitant, for she always seemed cautious but in control. Something spontaneous and unpredictable threw her off, and I took a secret pleasure in finding something I could do better than her.

A few meters down the path, coarse boulders gave way to bare dirt and loose rocks, and she slipped, gripping my hand with the great strength of fear seeking safety. Once steadied, she continued, but her descent was far more hesitant, for despite her willingness she was not at ease.

About two-thirds down a shelf of solid rock extended toward the Pacific, and I led her along this narrow flat bench. Once we rounded the promontory, the shelf widened. We were alone: no one above us on the lookout or below us on the beach could see us. Seeking a place hidden from anyone who happened to follow us, I clambered up the rocky slope, pulling her up behind me, and found a smooth rock ledge protected from prying eyes below by a massive boulder but exposed to the afternoon sun's warmth.

Unfolding the towels, I laid them one on top the other to cushion the hard surface and tugged her down beside me. "No one can see us here," I said.

"What about a drone?"

"We'd be hard to spot," I replied. "And there are no drones."

Opening her bag, I took out the water bottle and we quenched our thirst.

The white-flecked blue expanse of the Pacific attracted our attention for a time, but the temptation offered by our private aerie was irresistible.

Murmuring, "Let's start with dessert," I removed her kerchief, wig and sunglasses and kissed her, not lightly.

"Someone might see us," she protested.

"No one can see us," I countered.

"Are you sure?"

"Look for yourself," I said. "We're invisible."

Her discomfort was unassuaged and I said, "if we hear anything, it will take three seconds to pull up your tube top and pull down your skirt."

"What about you?"

"I'm sunbathing," I replied. "Nothing objectionable about that."

She let me kiss her, and I satisfied my curiosity about the difficulty of slipping her tube top down to her midriff. "You could do with some sun," I said, and that was the end of our conversation.

In other words, she allowed herself to be persuaded.

Our dreamy state of sunbathed embrace dissolved her modesty and the sun warmed us both until hunger prompted us to open her picnic lunch of salmon pate, cucumber-tomato sandwiches, peeled carrots and brownies embedded with dark chocolate pieces she'd baked that morning. Her picnic was beautifully made and packed, and it struck me anew that no small thing was done badly in her life.

"You're a natural in Nature," I joked, and she replied, "Sunbathing isn't supposed to be so active."

"Your brownies are exceptional, but your first dessert was beyond exceptional."

I expected a witty repartee, but she was quiet. Collecting the brownie crumbs on her napkin, she pressed them together and lifted the grains to her lips.

Turning to me, she took my hand and squeezed it almost as tightly as when she'd slipped on the treacherous trail.

"I don't know how to say this without sounding foolish, but you finding this place for us, being pressed against the warm rock, the sound of the waves below us… something happened, not just pleasure or happiness, but something changed in me, not just in my feelings but all of me. I can't describe it, but I feel it."

I had never heard her speak like this. Whatever she felt must have been as imperative as drawing breath.

"I can see it in you," I said, for something about her had changed, not just her manner or mood, and seeing her changed me, too, even though I couldn't describe exactly what had changed. The sensation reminded me of my dream before we met, when my dream-self was surprised to recall that we were already lovers.

Relaxing her grip on my hand, she turned to me and murmured, "It's strange, but I want you to understand, even though I don't understand it myself."

No other words came to me.

Certain moments are permanently captured by our minds, much like a photo. I don't mean traumatic events; I'm referring to moments of everyday life. We don't choose what is etched in this manner; they choose themselves. What our deepest self recognizes in these moments is not always clear. The images are etched in us but the full meaning remains elusive, emerging over time.

This was such a moment.

I remember her expression as if it were a photo imprinted in me by constant study. I felt her vulnerability and the uncertainties beneath her resolve, and the intensity of her life force.

Still gazing at me, she ventured, "You really love me, don't you?"

I smiled. "I'm happy you can tell."

"But how can you be sure you love me? Maybe you've just convinced yourself."

"No, I'm madly in love with you. It's not something you conjure up."

Lowering her gaze, she asked, "but what if there's a side to me you haven't seen?"

"You can have secrets, but not a secret self," replied. "The same goes for me."

She looked up and I asked, "What about you? Are you in love with me or did you convince yourself for some crazy reason?"

She didn't smile. "I was afraid that I was just convincing myself, for all the usual reasons—being lonely, wanting the thrill of falling in love, of being swept out of my little boxed-in life. That's why it took so long to approach you. I didn't trust my own feelings."

"And what did you conclude?"

"When our hands touched in The Black Cat, I felt a physical connection. Even though we were fighting, we clicked. You were so comfortable with yourself in my flat, so attentive to me, I could trust you."

"Does all that good stuff mean you love me?"

She punched me playfully on the shoulder. "You want me to say it out loud, don't you? Yes."

Puffball clouds drifting across the blue expanse momentarily blocked the sun, and the warmth faded as the afternoon breeze freshened. The warmth of our aerie kept us comfortable, but the waning day softened the sun and cooled the swirling air.

"I feel the clock ticking, and I hate it," I said. "What's to become of us?"

"I don't know," she said. "It was always going to end."

"Yes, but what about next year? Or five years from now? Couldn't things change for you?"

"Of course," she replied, but there was little hope in her voice.

Fearing her answer, I asked, "Do you have someone waiting for you at home? A husband, a lover, a fiancé, a child?"

She gave me a harsh look that softened. "I guess I would wonder the same thing if we switched places," she finally said. "That's the secret everyone keeps, right? 'I love you, darling, but I'm married. Oh, and I have a kid.' No, none of those."

"I can't help wanting an ordinary life with you where you're annoyed I overcooked the pasta."

Widening her eyes, she asked, "Do you hate overcooked noodles?"

"It ruins me," I replied.

"Maybe you'll be annoyed with me for overcooking the noodles."

"I can't see you overcooking noodles."

"That would be the least of our problems." Though she said it coyly, I detected a serious undertow.

The sun reappeared from behind the clouds, and I said, "Let's go down to the beach before it gets too cold."

She agreed and after packing up the towels, we retraced our steps and continued descending the uneven trail as the shadows lengthened. We reached the gray sand of the beach and exchanged greetings with the couple we'd seen as they began their ascent. We had the secluded cove all to ourselves.

Freed of the blond wig, her long hair swirled in the freshening breeze, and then trailed her as she began trotting down the damp gray sand left as the tide receded.

Her turning to beckon me is etched in my memory: the intimacy of her happiness, the tenderness of her gesture, her youthful vigor and life-force field, pulling me like gravity.

Some days, everything is right with the world. This was one of those days, and we both knew it. You don't want it to end even as you know it must.

The clouds dimmed the setting sun, and once we caught our breath, the wind felt arctic on our bare skin. Taking one last moment to enjoy the solitude of the cove, we held hands and gazed at the wealth around us: the foaming waves on the beach, the reddening sun, the rocky promontory with our hidden aerie, and the world we were forced to return to, of parking lots and destinations.

That romance blossoms, reaches a peak of dew-petaled vibrancy and then matures is inevitable, but the change was more sudden than I expected. It felt like abruptly dropping into a lower orbit where everything moved faster. We still met every night in the dimly lit apartment, we still found comfort and extravagance in our embraces, but the wistful futility of time advancing toward her departure weighed on us.

She spoke less, and so did I. I feared she would withdraw as a means of reducing the sorrows of parting, but she drew closer physically even as her verbal expressions ebbed.

I tried to prepare myself for our final moments together, at least in this time and place, but failed. Perhaps she sensed this, or felt the same way, for our last night together slipped past unnoticed in the anticipation of a dozen more ahead. This is how she planned it, and I can't fault her judgement that this was easier on us both.

The next night, as usual I confirmed the hallway was clear and approached her door. A white envelope with my initials was taped to the midnight-blue door. I knew at once it was her goodbye, and that she'd decided to avoid what we both dreaded.

The letter was brief, and in her hand, the same cursive block letters of her first note to me.

"Please forgive this ending. Please remember our time together and know it is the most important of my life. Please don't try to find me. That would only hurt us both. Christine."

Hers was a futile plea. Of course I would follow her and find her, and perhaps to ease my grief, I began plotting a journey to her Home Country.

It would not be particularly easy. For a variety of reasons, visitors were restricted to tightly controlled tour groups with guides and rigid itineraries. Independent travelers had to navigate a series of bureaucratic rapids.

I had no one to guide me, and so my first task was finding one.

Section Two

I took a break from the pen and paper, as The Little Lady heeled over so dramatically that the mast must have dipped into the hill-sized wave threatening to swamp us. At the last moment the old yacht gave a sickening shudder and righted herself—spared again. Then exhaustion took me and I slipped into the semi-delirium that passes for sleep out here.

To help me find a guide, I turned first to the eccentric bookstore owner who was plain-speaking and worldly,

Sitting behind his paper-strewn desk surrounded by precarious stacks of books, he looked like an aging elf who'd struck it rich in late middle-age and acquired a belly in enjoying his unexpected wealth. All his balding crown and untidy fringe of white hair needed was a peaked elfin hat, preferably forest-green.

I laid out my desire to visit Christine's Home Country and need for advice on how to get permission. He listened intently and then waved me to stop. "Yes, yes, crazy love, you must, you must, you must." Gesturing to a female employee passing by his glass-partitioned office, he said, "Talk to Rikki. She's been everywhere."

I'd seen her before, of course, in browsing the shelves, and knew she was competent and reliable, which is why the owner always rehired her when she returned from another of her travels. I'd heard that she knew several languages and had traveled extensively on three continents, which seemed appropriate, given that her bloodline likely mixed at least three continents.

She'd tied her hair up, and wore khaki trousers with pockets and a man's button-down Oxford shirt. She must have been in the cramped staff kitchen during her break, for the scent of fresh-squeezed limes cut through the musty old book-smell.

If she was amused or cynical about my travel plan, she suppressed it.

"To get permission as an independent traveler, you'll need a cultural or scientific sponsor," she said. "I was rejected until I found a customer here, a retired philosophy professor, who was willing to sponsor me. I can recommend you to him."

Her deep-brown eyes surveyed me, perhaps to see if I was up to the task. "There's also a couple of interviews," she continued, "which are basically polite interrogations. I've read they also do a background check. Rumor has it they use lie-detection software, which is why they record the interrogations."

My hopeful mood crashed. What would they think of a rabble-rousing activist? Probably much like Superman handling Kryptonite.

"If you get approved, you'll have an interpreter, who's also a minder to keep you out of trouble."

That would severely complicate my efforts to contact Christine.

"Who you get is a real crapshoot," she added. "You might get a pretty nice one like I did, or a real sourpuss."

Everything she said added obstacles to an impassable barrier.

"What about an obscure border crossing?"

She shook her head. "You'd need a work permit, which you won't be able to get without someone giving you a job, and you still need a visa,"

"How about sneaking across?"

This drew a faint smile. "You're not exactly going to blend in," she said wryly. "And without speaking the language, you'll be in trouble even before you're turned over to the local police."

Noting my downcast expression, she said, "You have a chance if you're sincere about whatever interest you have in the culture. Pick something you're actually passionate about, and your chances improve."

"What got you in?"

"I tried food, but everyone uses that, so it didn't work," she replied. "I'm interested in religions and rituals, so the Professor helped me make that officially acceptable."

The Professor was the key, and to get a measure of him I asked, "What kind of books does he buy?"

"Last time, he bought a couple manga, Melville's *The Confidence Man* and a mystery."

"What's he like?"

She paused and then smiled slightly. "Old, as in ancient, but not doddering. Unpretentious, lives alone but has a companion. They go shopping together; he cooks for her. He has a garden and makes vegetarian dumplings. He pan-fried some for me. He looks like just another old man, but he won the teaching prize at the university."

Taking a pen from one of her trouser pockets, she wrote a phone number and address on one of the store's giveaway bookmarks. "I'll talk to the Professor tonight; you can call him tomorrow. He's a bit of a night-owl so wait until mid-morning."

Thanking her profusely, I walked home in a state of scattering thoughts and conflicting emotions. What could I claim with credible sincerity was so core to me that it justified a visit to the Home Country? I doubted "overthrowing the tyranny of money" would make the desired impression.

And worst of all, I'm a lousy liar, and transparently so.

In other words, it seemed hopeless.

There was nothing to be done but visit the Professor, begging bowl in hand, and hope he could conjure up a way forward out of thin air.

The prospect—and the Professor—intimidated me. I was powerless and adrift, and I didn't like the feeling. I envied those who had supreme confidence that something would turn up, and all they had to do was wait for it to appear. I had no such confidence, and no evidence in my life that things turn up unbidden and without effort.

Maybe it was a lack of faith. But faith has to be sincere. Saying you have faith doesn't mean you actually have faith. I had no faith that doing nothing would manifest a reunion with Christine.

I also had no faith that a reunion would rekindle our happiness. She'd made it clear that her life had constraints that left no allowance for me. Though I was a fool, I wasn't fool enough to trust that everything would be restored if I could just see her again.

Maybe I no choice but to hope we still had a future together, as the alternative left me no future.

Hope may be a fragile kind of faith, one devoured by disappointment. I wanted the kind of faith that was impervious to disappointment, but this can't be willed into being, any more than we can will love into being. Christine feared she'd willed love into being, but that's hubris. We don't have that power. We can will an illusion of love or faith into being for a short time, but not real love or real faith.

These rambling, confused thoughts filled my mind and heart.

With a tightness in my throat I called the Professor the next day. His accented voice was cordial and he suggested dropping by his house at 10 pm that evening—late for most elderly but maybe early for a night owl.

I borrowed the work van and drove to his address in a tree-lined neighborhood of sturdy bungalows and large tidy yards. It was a desirable old neighborhood within walking distance of the university.

In other words, the ideal place for a subversive to hide.

The Professor's white-plank house had a steep-pitched roof and matching entry with a decorative pierced-metal light that dimly illuminated an arched front door mounted on heavy cast-iron hinges. The windows were dark. Next door, beyond a large tree separating the properties, a handsome house with an expansive porch was fronted by a modest illuminated sign that read The Theosophical Society.

In the faint glow cast by the entry light, I discerned a figure in the shadows of the tree, moving gracefully through a set of Tai Chi movements. The barefoot figure was clad in classic loose-fitting dark trousers and tunic. The steadiness of his limbs did not suggest old age and I wondered if a younger person had permission to practice Tai Chi in the Professor's yard. I waited until the figure completed his set before stepping out of the van and approaching the house.

The figure stepped out of the shadows and raised his hand in greeting. As my bookstore co-worker had said, he looked like any other old Asian man: slight build, thinning gray hair, age-worn features creased by a welcoming smile. What differentiated him was his straight-backed posture, the sureness of his step and the sharpness of his gaze. When he looked me over, I felt his keen but detached interest. I would not want to be prey in his field of vision.

We exchanged greetings and I followed him up the brick entry steps into the house. He turned on the living room light and I was surprised by his collection of riotously vivid movie posters from America, Europe and Asia. Very little wall space was left for any other decoration. On the low table beside a well-used easy chair, a bouquet of flowers in a plain-white vase scented the room with fragrant roses; it had the look of a collection gathered from a home garden, with sprigs of yellow buds and orange poppies.   Beside the vase lay a disorderly spread of books. I recognized Braudel's history of France with bookmarks in the last third of both thick volumes, a Maigret mystery and several Japanese manga.

Two bamboo kendo sticks were leaning against the wall by a dramatic poster for the martial arts classic *Come Drink with Me* emblazoned with bright-yellow Chinese characters. Curiosity overwhelming politeness. I picked up one of the sticks and swung it lightly to get a feel for its weight and balance.

The Professor had silently indulged my survey of his living room, but now he took up the other stick and with an impish grin swung it towards my head. I instinctively blocked the blow with my stick and the Professor countered with a low sweep aimed at my knees. His attack was quick but not forceful; if he'd landed a blow it would have stung but not hurt.

Since I'd had no formal training in swords or kendo, my reflexive defense was based solely on my late-night sparring with longer, sturdier bamboo poles.

Noting that I made no attempt to strike him, he said, "Don't be afraid of hurting me." I launched a half-hearted swing straight down on his head which he easily deflected, and he waved his hand in remonstrance. "Not that, a real one." Following his light, quick technique, I tried a few attacks which he foiled, and as I readied another attempt, he deftly evaded my tardy defense and his stick audibly slapped my thigh.

He paused, grinning, and said, "I hope you don't mind. Practice is how we learn."

Setting the stick back against the wall, he said, "Your instincts are good. That was great fun. It's not often I get to strike a guest."

Both our foreheads glistened with sweat, and he said, "Let's get something to drink and a snack."

His kitchen retained the original tile counters, painted wood cabinets and dining nook; only the appliances had been updated. The ceramic Kitchen Gods figurines—bearded sages in robes--adorning the window sill were covered with a film of dust but the pans and dishware were neatly stored. The use-blackened wok on the stovetop evidenced a working kitchen.

The Professor filled two paisley-decorated glasses with water, handed one to me and then busied himself with a frying pan and a plate of raw dumplings he pulled from the refrigerator.

"I made these this morning," he commented. "They're vegetarian, I hope you don't mind."

After the oil heated in the pan, he arranged the potstickers in a circular pattern and put the kettle on the back burner.

Turning to me, he said, "When you were first defending against my attacks, your reactions were natural and required no thought. That is the Tao in action."

Lowering the heat, he doused the potstickers with hot water and covered the bubbling pan with a glass lid that clouded with condensation.

"When I instructed you to attack, you began planning, and lost your instinctual rhythm. This broke the flow of the Tao."

I nodded, and he added, "We feel the Tao of defense much more easily than the Tao of attack. Every attack by an opponent is an opening for your attack. Defense and offense are one movement. This is the Tao that's difficult to attain." Grinning, he said, "That's why I couldn't pass up the chance to spar with you. I need more practice."

I'd read Taoist classics in a university philosophy class but could never connect the abstract to my own experience until now. The Professor was right; I'd had no time for thinking, I'd simply reacted based on my informal training and instinct. Once I overthought it, I faltered.

Lifting the lid, the professor prodded the potstickers and set the lid aside. Retrieving two plates from a cupboard, he handed them to me and said, "Chopsticks are on the table."

Once I'd set the table, he brought the sizzling pan, covered it with a plate and deftly flipped the pan over so the circles of potstickers were transferred to the plate. The bottom of each dumpling was a crispy golden brown, and setting the plate between us, he gestured to bottles of hot chili sauce, Chinese vinegar and soy sauce on the table.

I knew enough to serve him first and then myself. As we consumed the tofu-and-water chestnut filled dumplings, he asked the purpose of my visit to the Home Country. I entrusted him with the embarrassing truth: a hopeless love.

I said nothing specific about Christine. Her extreme caution had made me careful, and I waited to see if the Professor asked about her. I'm not a good liar and wasn't sure how to deflect inquiries without raising suspicions.

"That's good, a quest of the heart," he commented. Drizzling the chili sauce and vinegar over three of the glistening dumplings, he asked, "Are you so comfortable with her that it's a spiritual experience?"

No one had ever asked me such a question, nor had I ever thought about the comfort I felt with her as a spiritual experience.

"Yes, though I didn't realize it until you asked."

"That's good," he remarked, and then asked, "Where does she live?"

The question took me aback, as it was so obvious a starting point, yet I had no clue. She'd made sure there were no digital fingerprints of our relationship—no email, texts or photos--and when I'd asked for her real name, she'd demurred, saying it was better for us both if I didn't know. I had no starting point for an online search, and no known associates of hers to ask.

With great embarrassment, I confessed, "I don't know. She kept her home life confidential."

I was on edge, as not knowing where she lived was a red flag. Either she'd kept me in the dark for a reason—to keep me from discovering she was married, for example—or I was so naively infatuated I didn't even press her for the most basic personal information. Neither reflected well on me or my quixotic visit.

This was her intent, of course; the less I knew about her, the lower the risk of confidences being broken

If the Professor found this troubling—and who wouldn't? —he kept it to himself. His comment was matter-of-fact: "Your itinerary will have to be flexible."

Dividing the last of the savory green-onion flecked dumplings between us, he said, "Now tell me what you do for a living, and what subjects you studied in university."

My university studies were another source of embarrassment, as I'd moved from one interest to another, racking up credits in architecture, biology, Korean poetry, economics, literature, philosophy and several stabs at Asian and Latin languages.

Glancing up from his plate, the Professor asked, "What will you say is the reason for your visit?"

A third embarrassment loomed. "I have no idea, though I've been thinking of nothing else."

"It's better to have an open mind than become attached to a bad idea," he said.

After praising his dumplings—certainly the most flavorful vegetarian potstickers I could recall—I gathered up the dishes and went to the sink to wash them. Afterward, he poured us each a slug of clear firewater from a squat ceramic bottle and we returned to the living room.

The firewater was high-proof and smelled slightly floral.

Tasting the liquor appreciatively, he asked, "Would you like to hear my suggestions?"

"Very much so."

"First, don't hide anything or lie. These will be detected and you will not get permission."

That was problematic, for I'd have to hide the real reason for my visit.

"Second, provide an explanation which accounts for the facts they can confirm, but in a way that reflects positively on the country and its political leadership."

In other words, it would be like going undercover.

"Third, choose a reason that you can be enthusiastic about. This is what will impress them the most—sincere enthusiasm."

Downing his remaining firewater with one swallow, the Professor continued. "Is your interest in architecture sincere?"

I hadn't thought about it, but explained that there was a time when I'd applied for admission to the school of architecture. I'd been rejected only because I lacked the required math credits.

"That's good," he remarked. "You also studied religions and philosophies, and so an interest in temples and churches is natural, isn't it?"

Though it would never had occurred to me, the pairing made a certain kind of sense. I could imagine dredging up an interest in visiting ancient temples and churches that had survived the turmoil of time.

"I would never have thought of it, but yes, that would be interesting."

Gazing at me, he asked, "Is there anything worrisome they might uncover about you?"

My caution—call it paranoia if you wish—reared up. The only things I knew about Christine were her father was a bigshot politician and that bad things would happen if our affair became public. But why this was so remained a mystery.

Unless she'd exaggerated the need for secrecy for private reasons—something I'd considered but rejected because her anxiety was so intense and her care so obsessive—then the discovery of our relationship would likely monkey-wrench my visa application and cause her problems—what kind I didn't know, but serious enough to make her anxiety the backdrop of our time together.

"No, no surprises," I replied. "I'm very conventional. I worry that my rabble-rousing for a new financial system will kill my chances."

He pondered this for a moment and said, "You care about the common people, and think a new way of issuing money would help them. I don't think that would be too controversial. It shows you have a kind heart. Your paid job is at a bookstore."

Warming to the subject, he added, "In your interview, mention the great wealth of religious buildings that deserve to be World Heritage sites, and the rich history of the country you wish to explore and share."

I was getting a feel for why the Professor's sponsorship generated successful applications.

"I'm giving you an Asian name," he announced. Arising from his chair, he went to a compact rolltop desk in the corner. I followed and watched him write a character on an index card. "This means sincerity, an honest heart, a truthful heart. In Japanese, it's pronounced Makoto."

By coincidence, a poster for a Japanese film occupied the space above the desk, and he saw it had caught my eye. Judging by the clothing and actress's hairstyle, it was from the 1950s.

"That's one of my favorite films, Ozu's *Late Spring*." The Professor commented. "I suggest watching it with *Early Summer*, which you may find relates to your situation."

His suggestion left me feeling the Professor had divined much more about me that I had about him. I'd never seen these films, and was naturally curious about the parallel he discerned to my life.

"There is no guarantee of success," he cautioned me. "If your sincerity is found wanting, your application will be denied."

Something about his statement made me ask, "If you don't mind me asking, why are you allowed to sponsor visitors?"

He fixed his detached gaze on me and his expression softened into amusement. "Academic exchanges make everyone look good. I suppose I'm seen as a useful contact."

Opaque bureaucracies and shadowy authority naturally prompt skepticism, and I wondered, useful in what way, and to whom? Maybe it was all as innocent as it seemed: a kindly retired academic helps independent travelers navigate a tricky visa approval process. But there were other possibilities. Perhaps the Professor actually had the power to grant permission, and the bureaucratic obstacle course was there to keep the riff-raff out.

Or maybe he was useful in ways only insiders could understand.

In other words, sincerity cuts two ways. The Professor seemed sincere to me, but self-interest isn't always transparent. He knew my motives, but I didn't know his.

It also occurred to me that perhaps there were two tracks invisible to applicants: one for typical independent travelers and another for those who might prove useful beyond a boost to tourism. Maybe that was part of the Professor's job as sponsor, to select the applicant's track.

This concerned me, because in revealing my true reason for wanting a visa, I'd raised red flags that no one could ignore. Could anyone be so foolish, to seek a woman in a foreign land without even knowing where she lived? Wasn't it obvious she didn't want him to know?

Putting myself in the Professor's shoes, I could imagine two possible explanations: the applicant (me) was delusionally lovelorn, intent on a quest that could only end in failure, or this absurd quest masked another purpose for my visit.

He'd taken me at my word without visible skepticism. In the Professor's shoes, I would have suggested the applicant (me) first get the woman's address before starting the visa process. Did it really not matter that my plan made no sense?

Or maybe I was needlessly muddying clear water, and he was simply a retired academic helping applicants, regardless of their motivations. He saw I was delusionally lovelorn but was trying to help me anyway.

In any event, he was the only portal open in an impassable barrier.

Walking me to the door, the Professor instructed me to complete the application and then send the draft for his review. Thanking him for feeding and helping me, I left with a feeling that the burdens weighing on me had lightened and become more complicated at the same time. The Professor was guiding my moves in a game where I didn't know the rules. I knew the consequences of losing and the rewards of winning, but nothing else.

*   *   *

At the Professor's behest, I began researching temples and churches in and around major cities, so once I located Christine I could travel to her home town with a plausible cover story.

The research was less arduous than I anticipated. The Portuguese had built churches, and a few had survived the wars and revolutions. A few Taoist temples had evaded fire and wanton destruction, as well as some very old Buddhist temples. All were architecturally worthy of study, reflecting the zeitgeist and technology of their era. Many were beautiful in craftsmanship and design, along classic *pattern language* lines. A handful of modern churches and temples were also worth a visit.

As you know by now, I'm not a skilled writer, so the Professor trimmed my verbosity to short, clear statements along the lines he'd suggested.

I received an interview slot faster than anticipated and agonized over what to wear as if it was a job interview. Thugs always wear suits when they appeared in court, and their defense attorneys must suggest that for a reason, so I wore the same jacket and tie borrowed from my roommate for my outing with Christine.

Telling myself not to fret didn't work. I had no experience in interrogations and couldn't fake a calm I didn't feel.

The applicants traveling in tours were queued outside a windowless one-story warehouse. The far fewer independent travelers were screened in a two-story building with well-maintained leafy landscaping, deep-set divided-pane windows and a gurgling tiled fountain in the cobbled courtyard. In contrast to the crowed warehouse, only a few visitors went about their business.

The interior was equally charming; this was obviously where the senior staff worked.

The female receptionist directed me to a room on the second floor. The large windows lining the stairwell and corridor were open to a welcome breeze, and it seemed an incongruously pleasant place for an interrogation that decided my fate.

The Asian interviewer greeted me cordially and I sat down facing him. He wore a standard white shirt and narrow dark tie, and his hair was neatly trimmed. I put his age as late 30s, a few years older than me. A camera sat on the desk beside him, and he adjusted it to point at my face. "We record every interview, it's standard practice," he assured me. "Please look into the camera when speaking."

As Nikki had warned me, this enabled screening applicants for micro-changes in facial expressions that indicated untruths. Could I perform a mind trick and forget Christine? I doubted this was possible.

I nodded acknowledgement and noticed a mirror on the side wall, bracketed by paintings of lushly forested rural villages, and reckoned it was a one-way mirror for observing applicants. This was of a piece with the surveillance Christine described: the Home Country took no half-measures.

The interviewer's first question must have sent the lie-detection software ablaze. "Do you know anyone from our country?"

My mind went blank and then I blurted, "Yes, my sponsor, the Professor."

"Anyone else?"

"Not by name," I replied. "Someone might have attended a meeting with me, but I don't even know their name." This much was true. I didn't know Christine's real name.

The interviewer glanced at what was likely a script and asked, "Do you feel friendly toward my country?"

"Absolutely. That's why I want to go there."

"Tell me about your political work." Clearly, they'd already done a background check.

I'd anticipated defusing this particular bomb by following the Professor's suggestion. "It's not actually political," I explained. "I don't follow parties or politicians. The idea is that another form of money would help everyone and the government, by giving everyone more money."

His next question got straight to the point. "Are you anti-government?"

"Absolutely not," I replied. "The government's job is to help people, and our financial proposal helps both the people and the government."

"If you have a positive experience in my country, would you be willing to share your experiences with others?"

It was a seemingly innocent question that hinted at a two-track process as I'd imagined: are you potentially useful to us? If so, you get fast-tracked. If not, you're rejected.

"Of course," I gushed. "I'd be delighted to share my experiences."

He took this enthusiasm in stride and moved to the next series of questions.

"You work at a bookstore," he noted. "Why your sudden interest in religious architecture?"

I'd also practiced a response to this line of inquiry. "It's not actually sudden," I explained. "I almost went to architecture school in university. The only reason I didn't is I was short of math credits."

I'd addressed him and he reminded me to look at the camera when answering.

"Sorry," I said. "As for my interest in religious architecture, my interest goes way back. I did a paper in university on the new cathedrals in Los Angeles and Oakland."

This wasn't strictly factual, but I had written a paper referencing the new cathedrals in their urban environment.

"Even then," I continued, "I thought some of the historic temples and churches in your country deserved to be World Heritage Sites. It's appalling that none of the historically important and beautiful temples and churches in your country have been properly recognized and valued."

The interviewer's bland expression responded subtly to this impassioned statement, and I added a few examples from my recent research to show that my interest was legitimate.

"How did you get the money for your proposed travel?"

The questions seemed to be designed to come from unexpectedly blunt directions to catch applicants off guard.

"I live very frugally," I replied. "I've been saving for years for this trip of a lifetime." The frugality and savings were true and easily confirmed by looking at our group house and my few possessions.

"Did you meet a woman from our country at one of your rallies?"

My skin tingled with this confirmation that the surveillance on Christine was extraordinarily thorough. A response came to me after a moment's hesitation, which I attributed to searching my memory. "Oh, right. That was our photographer, not me. An Asian woman asked him to take a few photos of her in front of city hall. He mentioned it in passing."

"You didn't meet her?"

Once again, the lie-detection software must have gone off the chart as I replied, "He pointed her out, that's all."

Struggling to maintain my composure, I told myself their interest in Christine's presence at our rallies was natural because she routinely attended. They would naturally wonder why and watch her closely. My friend and I were of similar height and build, so maybe her watchers had confused us.

"Have you ever been to The Black Cat club?"

I uttered a silent oath. How did they trace her to The Black Cat? Given the care she took, the likeliest explanation was they had an inside informant. In any event, a lie wouldn't fly; for all I knew, they had surveillance footage of the entrance. I replied," Yes, once, at the invitation of an artist who has a sculpture in the club."

I would have to contact Marianne and ask her to confirm my story should anyone ask. I reckoned the Home Country authorities would use local proxies to handle their inquiries to avoid raising any suspicions. But I'd planned to visit Marianne anyway, for another reason.

Placing a slip of paper in front of me, the interviewer asked, "Have you ever been to this address?"

It was Christine's building, and I suppressed the fear they knew everything and were just toying with me. "I don't know, what is it?"

As he wordlessly placing a photograph of the building's street frontage in front of me, I searched for a simple reason for having been there. "Oh, the laundromat, right. I sometimes go through the laundromat's back door as a shortcut to street parking in the back. There's a cinema down the street and parking's hard to find." I'd never actually done this at the laundromat, but I'd certainly taken similar shortcuts.

My interviewer made a show of studying my file, and I thought, well, at least I know they've be watching me closely. That they knew I'd been to Christine's club and building were two coincidences too many. In their shoes, I'd be as suspicious, too. Maybe my responses ramped their suspicions even higher.

Or maybe they had nothing better to do. In a crew of carpenters, everything starts looking like a nail to pound down.

It was possible that Christine had told them everything under duress. Or she might have offered an explanation salted with a few facts as a cover story. But if they'd known about us, the interviewer would be laying down photos of us together, not building facades.

In other words, they were on a fishing expedition, and I'd wriggled off the hooks.

My interviewer closed my file and said, "We'll be in touch."

Thanking him, I exited the room with relief mixed with uncertainty. Had I really done as well as I thought, or was everything I'd said just a clumsy pointer to an inept liar? Whether they knew about us or merely had suspicions, either way it would serve their interests to let me visit the Home Country and follow me there. If there was a connection between me and Christine, I would make my way to her. If there was no connection, that would soon be apparent.

Was I really worth all this attention? Obviously not. But Christine was clearly worth all this attention, and that's what impressed me. Something about her was dynamite wrapped around a chunk of plutonium.

* * *

I'd also been beavering away on my other project, locating Christine. My first step was asking Coltrane for the email address Christine had given him. It had been closed the day she left. No surprise there.

I also dropped by Marianne's warehouse studio to ask her to confirm my story of her inviting me to The Black Cat, and confiding my love for Christine and my plan to find her.

"I'm not sure that's wise," she counseled. "Christine kept all that private for a reason."

"Yes, I know. But I want to know why. Asking me to just forget her isn't going to work. Do you have a contact phone or email for her?"

"They were local and the accounts have been closed."

"If you don't mind me asking, did Christine take that sculpture of Asian Liberty with her?"

"Yes," Marianne replied. "She'd commissioned it, it was hers."

"Was she the model?"

Marianne guffawed. "She told me you'd come around asking that. Yes, she was the model. I suggested it, and at first she refused, but I said it should be her, so she eventually agreed."

Smiling grimly at Christine's predictive powers, I nodded. "I'm glad you insisted."

After a pause, I said, "I just went through an interrogation to get an independent traveler visa. These guys were watching Christine's every step. If someone happens to ask why I was here, tell them it was to ask you to design something for our next rally."

She gave me a dubious look and I added, "It won't be a guy who looks like a spy. It will be someone you know."

Taken aback, she glanced around the studio. "I'm afraid you'll endanger her poking into her private life."

"That's one possibility," I said, "but I might be the only one who's willing to run into a burning building to save her, too."

She gave me a look I couldn't interpret and then patted my shoulder. "Crazy love will win out."

I 'd previously considered visiting The Black Cat to ask about Christine but that had been revealed as a nest of informants. Presuming she'd actually attended the university, her records were confidential, so that was a dead end. I was down to her apartment manager, and that was problematic. Not only was her information confidential, a man inquiring about an attractive young woman smacked of stalking. I needed a reason for the manager to believe he was helping Christine by sharing her real name and address in her Home Country.

Another troubling possibility had occurred to me. Maybe she hadn't returned home but had gone to ground somewhere else in the U.S. I couldn't think of any way to confirm or deny this possibility. It would be just like me to go off on a wild goose chase thousands of miles away while Christine was actually only 100 kilometers away. For all I knew, she may have fled to another continent.

But given her explanation of having only a few months' respite in America, it seemed far more likely that she'd returned home to the duties that she'd described as unbreakable.

After rejecting various alternatives, I concluded the approach most likely to succeed with the building manager was to show him my friend's photographs of Christine and explain that she'd asked him to take the photos but the email she'd given him no longer worked. As a favor to her, we wanted to mail her the photos, and could he share her name and address?

Since she'd left the country, stalking was not an issue, and what reason would he have to deny such a harmless request? I could show him the photos and her handwritten email address so he could confirm it was her and her writing.

This was my one chance, as coming back with another ploy if he turned me away would instantly arouse his suspicions.

To increase the credibility of my story, I dragged Coltrane along with me, having confessed my relationship with Christine and my plan to visit her. A decent dinner out was a sufficient bribe, and after confirming the manager was onsite, we trudged up the steps to his third floor flat.

The manager was so thin that though his belt was pulled tight, his trousers still threatened to slip off his hips. Smoothing his thinning hair with a harried gesture, he listened distractedly to my story and glanced at the photo and email. "Yup, that's her," he noted. "Didn't see much of her after she rented the two apartments."

Two apartments? Containing my shock, I said as off-handedly as I could manage, "She lived in the one down the hall."

"She also rented the one next door," he said. "Month to month. Now I have two to rent."

"I know you're busy but you'd be doing her a favor if you'd help us send her the photos she wanted."

With visible reluctance he shuffled to a filing cabinet and extracted a file labeled with each apartment number. "She was no trouble, that's for sure. Paid on time, no complaints. Hang on a second, I'll find her application for you."

At that moment a bearded youth knocked on his half-open door and said, "Sorry, my toilet's running again, and rattling the handle doesn't stop it. Could you come down and look at it?"

"Lordy-Lord-Lord, what a day," he mumbled, and handing me the file he said, "You fellas wait in the hall until I get back."

Once the pair had headed down the staircase, I took out my phone and quickly snapped photos of every page in Christine's file: her passport—her face expressionless with her hair pulled back in a tight ponytail—her handwritten application, deposit receipt, and a payment for work performed in her adjacent apartments.

I had her real name and her home address, and that felt like an immense victory.

The manager trudged up the steps and shook his head. "The chain fell off the handle again," he explained, and then opened the door to his flat. Handing him the file, I thanked him and asked if we could see the two open apartments, as I was thinking of moving out of my group house.

The prospect of renting one of the flats lifted his spirits and he said, "You need good credit, a couple of references and a recent paystub."

"I have all three," I assured him, and as Coltrane rolled his eyes at our delayed exit, we followed the manager to the apartment I'd visited, the one she'd said was a friend's that she was using in her absence.

The rooms looked small and forlorn, even though they'd been freshly painted. The black bedroom was now white. "The walls in here were black," I commented, and the manager said, "Yup. You know the trick to covering black paint? Put a coat of silver paint on it first as a primer."

Her vacant rooms ruined me, and I welcomed satisfying my curiosity about the apartment she'd rented next door. It too was freshly painted, and shared the same floor plan only flipped, so the bedrooms shared the same wall.

I opened the bedroom closet to give an appearance of interest and saw a drywall patch about one meter square in the wall shared by both bedroom closets. It was in the lower corner along the floor, and the manager commented, "Funny thing about that patch, it's like she cut a hole between the apartments."

"Who lived here?" I asked, and he shrugged. "Nobody, as far as I know. She said she needed it as a guest room, but I never saw any guests."

Her subterfuge about using a friend's flat and the secret passage suddenly made sense. This apartment was her official home that was watched and probably bugged. Once the lights were out, she could put on some white-noise music and sneak through the closets to the apartment I knew, the one where she could live free of surveillance for at least a few hours at night.

It was clever, and it offered me a window on just how far she'd gone to create a private life. I'd shared a small slice of that private life, but just how small I could only guess.

*   *   *

There was no way to confirm Christine still lived at the address on her passport. I could easily imagine her maintaining an official address but living incognito elsewhere. But it was a start.

My friend Coltrane had recruited a young native speaker to search for Christine on social media and the web, but as I expected, even her real name drew a blank. I'd hoped she kept a social media account as many people do, to project a façade of normalcy, but there was nothing but her name in a class list from her high school days. All digital fingerprints had been meticulously wiped clean.

I'd heard nothing from the Home Country visa office, and so naturally I worried that my half-truths and anxiety had torpedoed my application. I considered calling the Professor to ask him to put in a good word, but that smacked of desperation. If he'd recommended "no" I wasn't going to change his mind, and if he'd recommended "yes" he'd done all he could.

As a backup plan, I scoured guided tour itineraries with the idea of getting to her city and then slipping away from the tour to find her address. I'd probably be able to manage that with a taxi ride, but if she wasn't there, it would only be a matter of time before authorities caught up with me. I couldn't register at a hotel without a proper visa, so where would I hide? It was a poor alternative, but the only one available.

Since Rikki had mentioned being interviewed twice, I wasn't overly surprised to get a second appointment at the visa office, and I took it as a positive sign that my application was still in the queue.

My second interview was on the same floor of the courtyard building but in a different room, with a matronly middle-aged woman with short hair dyed jet-black who greeted me with a smile. Prepared for another round of probing questions about my contact with Christine, I was relieved that this interview documented my itinerary and the specific sites I wanted to visit. I'd already adjusted my route to start in Christine's city and proceed from there, and this choice was easy to justify as there were significant churches and temples in the city that anyone with my claimed interest would want to see.

I'd warmed to my research, not only to show sincere interest but as a distraction from my doubts. The odds of me locating her anywhere but her official address were essentially zero, and given the confidential layers of her life I doubted it would be that easy. If she kept two flats here, why not three there?

And Marianne's warning plagued me in the early morning hours. Christine had carefully organized her life to protect each element from the others. If any two broke through her containment, they might set off a chain reaction and destroy whatever she was protecting.

Marianne was right: I was trying to insert myself in her life against her wishes.

But did she really think she could unleash a crazy love and then banish it? Wasn't it hubris to think you could move others around the board to suit your needs without regard for what they felt? Didn't everyone have an equal serving of will?

And what's the most accurate description for an attractive woman inviting a man to a private club and then taking him home to make love that night in her arty bedroom? Seduction comes to mind, doesn't it? Yes, our attraction was magnetic and our emotions real, but had her decisions been made with me in mind? I was part of her plan, not the other way around.

In other words, if you light a fire, don't expect to control the conflagration.

At a minimum, she owed me an explanation. I would accept the truth, however painful, but nothing less.

Then there was the money. I had some savings, but my paltry pay didn't allow much to set aside. My only valuable possession was a vintage guitar I'd bought from a friend years ago, but even selling that would leave only a barebones budget. With great reluctance I took Christine's cashier's check to my bank and deposited it. As she'd said, the check was good and I suddenly had five year's pay in my account.

Rather than be elated, I felt guilty. This was supposed to be a gift accepted only in dire circumstances, and I was taking it to disrupt her life.

* * *

The cliché is things happen in threes. I just didn't expect the third to be so different from the first two.

To my great elation, I received an email confirming the approval of my application for independent travel in the Home Country in the morning. Never mind why, all that mattered was I had a visa granting me independent travel.

A short time later, I received approval of my itinerary. This gave me what I wanted: permission to go to Christine's city first. I immediately booked the next available flight to the Home Country.

The third thing would arrive on much darker wings the day before I left.

Coltrane called and said, "I've got something you have to see" His voice implied it wasn't something nice, and he refused to elaborate. I awaited his arrival at our group house with vibrating impatience.

He arrived looking grim. I escorted him into my room and closed the door. He opened his laptop and said, "You know the young guy I recruited to look for Christine online? Someone sent him one of those amateur sex videos that people make fun of, and here's what he noticed."

Coltrane opened the video and I had a sinking feeling of dreadful anticipation. The camera appeared to be fixed on a tripod by a window and captured a large white-walled room barren of decoration with two double beds, a nightstand covered with liquor bottles and plastic cups between the beds and a few cushioned chairs along the rear wall. The audio quality was poor and the images grainy. The video was clearly raw and unedited, because nothing much was going on.

Naked men and women, all Asian, were listlessly lounging on the beds and chairs. The men were potbellied and middle-aged, the women were young, slim and attractive. One young woman was perfunctorily performing oral sex on one of the men sprawled on the second bed. A paunchy man stood by the window smoking a cigarette. Judging by the swirl of the smoke, either the window was partially open or an air conditioning vent was above the window.

Christine, her long hair down, slumped cross-legged on a chair against the rear wall, toying with a plastic cup. She was naked, like everyone else.

Coltrane paused the video and zoomed in on her face. "I'd given my friend one of the photos I took of Christine, and he digitized it to run facial recognition software, in the hopes he could find a photo of her somewhere on social media. The software confirmed this match."

I didn't need software to recognize Christine's face and body.

Against my will, I was trembling. To say I was in shock is an understatement.

Coltrane gauged my reaction and said, "I'm really sorry, but I knew you'd want to know,"

Drained of life, I said, "Yes, thank you," and my rational mind clicked through possible explanations. None were attractive. She was willing: unattractive. She was coerced: worse.

"I know it's painful, but you need to watch the first part," Coltrane explained. "There are a few things that could be clues to the location."

Even without Coltrane's urging, I was compelled to watch, to satisfy my curiosity and wring out every drop of misery. Even with the sound level pushed to maximum, voices were still muffled and occasionally inaudible. The whole thing was depressingly unstimulating. No wonder videos like this were distributed for purposes of mockery.

A shrill female voice cut through the lethargy and the camera swung round to the room's entrance to focus on a young woman with hair almost as long as Christine wearing a cowboy hat. She laughed loudly and poked the nearest potbellied male with the end of a whip. Stripping to her underwear and a wispy negligee, she pushed the man to his knees and then sat astride his back, encouraging him to carry her forward with lively orders and whip.

As the camera followed her progress toward the beds, the previously listless participants perked up, the men exchanging jokes while the women giggled. Christine was now off-camera.

Once the cowgirl reached the second bed, she dismounted, audibly slapping her ride's flabby derriere and pushed the woman off the supine man. Judging by the laughter, she must have derided his manliness, and mounting him with mock enthusiasm, she went through a vigorous pantomime of passionate completion before sidling off and making comments that brought forth guffaws from the onlookers.

She then pulled the young woman sitting on the bed to her feet and kissed her hard, squeezing her with exaggerated glee.

In other words, the life of the party.

In this momentary silence of her kiss, a bell rang faintly in the background, followed by a second bell with a slightly different tone. The ringing continued but was soon drowned out by the participants' voices. Coltrane repeated the segment, commenting, "Those are church bells."

Coltrane restarted the video, and as the cowgirl started a pillow fight aimed at the men, someone lifted the camera tripod to move it closer to the action. In the process of being lifted, the camera swung past the window at an odd angle, revealing an aluminum mullion dividing two large windows. The brief view through the windows was a blur, but a plaza and trees surrounded by office towers could be discerned.

Coltrane stopped the video. "See that plaza? That might help you pin down the location. I'll send you the audio clip of the bells and this one of the view outside."

The off-angle view of the plaza as the camera swung round wasn't much to go on, but with the two church bells in mind, I suddenly recognized the location: this plaza fronted a landmark 19th century cathedral with two spired bell towers. This architecturally and historically significant monument was naturally already on my itinerary.

It was in this moment of fractured suffering that I discerned the presence of fate, or perhaps destiny, in my decision to reunite with Christine. Against long odds, I'd gained permission to visit as an independent traveler. I'd obtained her official address, but nothing else. Now, practically at the last minute, a glimpse of at least one location in her private life was revealed to be within a stone's throw of a place I was already scheduled to visit.

These coincidences didn't seem coincidental, and my distraught tumult was leavened, however slightly, by the recognition of forces larger than my will, or hers.

He closed the laptop and I felt drained. Trying to keep my voice flat, I asked, "Is there more?"

"Nothing with any more clues," he replied, and his clipped tone strongly implied there was nothing to be gained from watching the rest.

"How bad was it for her?"

He shrugged. "Not that bad. Some girl-on-girl stuff, a little punishment. Pretty tame and other than Cowgirl, pretty lame."

"Not exactly what the naïve boyfriend hoped to see," I replied. "Maybe lame, but still humiliating."

He exhaled loudly and said, "That was the point, wasn't it? You sure you want to go to all this trouble to find out what's going on? She's not there by choice and you're not going to change that."

That was exactly what I was going to do. I just didn't know how.

Section Three

It's morning in the mid-Pacific, though not a bright and cheerful one. We can't tell if the typhoon is weakening or the edge of the storm's eye is passing over us. It's not getting worse, so that means it's getting better. At least that's what I tell myself.

After moving the cathedral up to the top of my list, I spent my last hours researching video and maps of the buildings around the plaza. An unremarkable four-story building of white-painted plaster looked like the most likely site of the camera, on the third or fourth floor. Short of staking out the entry in the hopes of spotting Christine, I wasn't sure the information would be of any use. The location might have been used only once, and even if it was used regularly, there was no way to know if Christine would be there. The time stamp of the video was a previous Sunday, and I was arriving late Thursday and scheduled to visit the church the following day, Friday. If the gathering was a weekly affair, my timing was auspicious.

The claustrophobic logjam clogging my mind left little opening for sleep, and I returned again and again to the humiliation imposed on Christine and how painful this must be for her. To be a subjugated sex toy was humiliation for any human, but for a bright, bold, beautiful woman, well-educated and wealthy, it was the ultimate degradation. This was obviously the intention of the flabby functionaries who had some hold on her so powerful that her bigshot father—presuming that was true—could not save her.

It was painful for another reason, too, of course; seeing the woman I desired and loved used for someone else's cruel amusement was a devilish agony.

My rage at the flabby functionaries had no boundaries, and I struggled not to let my intense craving for revenge cloud my critical thinking, for I needed a plan, one that I could manage in a foreign city with an interpreter-minder dogging me every step of the way.

Fogged by hurt, shock and exhaustion, with great effort I worked out the fundamentals of a plan. The first step was the obvious one, visiting her official address to see if she still lived there. I could try to slip away my first night via cab, but since I didn't speak the language, that might not settle the matter if someone other than Christine answered the door. If I wanted the services of my interpreter, I'd have to hope he'd accept a bribe and keep his mouth shut, or have a cover story innocuous enough for him to agree to the detour.

Given his job was holding the reins of foreigners, I reckoned a bribe would be more likely to get me deported than be of any help.

As for an innocuous cover story, my only connection to the Home Country was the Professor, and I reckoned I could ask if he had any relatives who could plausibly be at Christine's official address. The problem was officialdom could easily detect the ploy by searching residence permits and other records, for everyone had to have permission to change residences or travel. I saw no way around this obstacle and sought another solution.

The only other option was recruiting an English-speaking native from the hotel staff to aid me. This required enough money to win their cooperation, but not enough to arouse suspicion that I was involved in illegal activities. Honesty had the merit of sincerity; I could simply say I was looking for a friend I met in the States but wasn't sure her address was current.

On the other hand, hotel staff were likely obligated to report anything foreign guests requested other than hotel services, so that was also a risky gambit.

One way or another, I needed to confirm she lived there or not. If not, I could move on to the building fronting the church plaza.

The most likely source of information would be workers in and around the building who might have seen her and who might be persuaded with cash to reveal the location of the suite.

Alternatively, I might fail to find anyone who'd seen her, which meant the sex party had been a one-off. If I couldn't pick up some other lead, my inquiries would be dead in the water.

If someone had seen her, my next problem was gaining access to the suite, and for that I'd need a key, borrowed from maintenance staff. The ubiquity of bribes made offering cash incentives unremarkable, and so the sticking point was the cover story: it had to be ordinary and arouse sympathy. Affairs of the heart qualified, especially since I could describe mine with such pained sincerity.

Beyond these two leads, I had nothing.

As I noted at the start, most things fail, and given the paucity of my leads, my foolish expedition could be expected to fail. My one frayed hope was the intervention of fate or destiny: there were too many favorable coincidences to declare it all chance. And so I'd have to put my faith in *something will happen*, something which I could not foresee that would break the logjam.

* * *

As Rikki had observed, being assigned an interpreter (whose services we paid for, of course) was from both the visitor's and the interpreter's points of view, a crapshoot. It was a gamble both my interpreter and I lost, as the fellow holding the card with my name on it at the exit from customs was unsmiling and dour, as if he's just lost a packet at the casino of life. If not for his haircut—the barber had apparently placed a large ramen bowl over his head and snipped any hair below the rim—he was a fine-looking fellow, tall, well-built enough to be either ex-military or familiar with weight training. He wore conventional dark slacks and white shirt, with a bit of flair added by a red and gold silk tie.

He was not effusive. My guess was either he was hung over or he disapproved of me and perhaps his job.

He glanced at the worn bag slung over my shoulder and I detected a slight increase in his general air of disapproval: he was probably thinking; oh great, another no-tip budget foreigner.

Reckoning there was no harm in trying to make a positive first impression, I said, "I won't be a bother. I'm sure we'll have a good time together."

"Hundred percent," he remarked without enthusiasm, and I interpreted this cryptic utterance to mean a good time was guaranteed. His delivery reduced the sincerity of the guarantee by approximately one hundred percent.

It did provide my private nickname for him: Mr. Hundred-Percent.

He ordered a taxi on his phone and we briefly discussed security measures and the next few days' itinerary. Repeating the instructions issued by the visa office, independent travelers were not allowed to modify their own phones to work in the Home Country, and we were required to carry our officially provided phones (which we rented, of course) at all times. This was obviously to keep track of us, though the ubiquitous public security cameras also tracked everyone via biometric recognition. He summarized all this curtly: "If you're caught without your phone, you'll get in trouble."

I'd decided to try anesthetizing Mr. Hundred-Percent by overloading him with information. In other words, I would be the Teacher's Pet who didn't just carry my phone, I would raise my hand and volunteer my every move. So I prattled on about why I wanted to see the cathedral first; it was an architectural gem, historically important, it would be a World Heritage site in any other country, and so on. It think it's fair to say I pushed his boredom level to hundred percent.

Citing a very real exhaustion from the rigors of travel, I asked to be dropped at my hotel.

With an air of disinterest, he asked, "Would you like a female companion tonight?"

The offer stank of entrapment and I replied, "That's very kind of you, but no thank you."

"Don't go looking on your own," he said in a flat tone. "You'll get in trouble. And if you get in trouble, I get in trouble."

"I understand," I replied. "If I want companionship, I'll let you know."

We rode in silence to the hotel and I exited with a strained smile. Mr. Hundred-Percent would not be offering me a very high percentage of joy, and posed more of an obstacle than I'd anticipated. I suspected he'd been selected to not just keep close tabs on a dubious foreigner but to trip me up.

As he said, hundred percent.

*   *   *

Given that the hotel catered to independent travelers, I concluded the staff would report anything untoward, even if they accepted a bribe. So approaching staff was out. That left civilians chosen at random, an option that was much too risky to be optimal. Given the security measures on independent travelers, trying to take a taxi on my own would likely raise alarm bells. Cabs and drivers were undoubtedly monitored, so I'd need a local to order the taxi. I also reckoned I was less likely to trigger an alarm if I was with locals. So far as I could tell, friendships had yet to be banned,

Despite my exhaustion, this first night was the best opportunity to check on Christine's official address. I needed a local to accompany me in case whomever answered the door wasn't Christine and they didn't speak English.

To feign staying in my hotel room all night, I showered, put on the white bathrobe provided and ordered room service, making sure to greet the smartly uniformed server effusively and tip him generously, so if he make a report it would positive. Assuming the rooms were bugged, I sent a text to Mr. Hundred Percent wishing him a good night, placed my phone on the nightstand, clicked on the TV to the English language channel and lowered the volume. After closing the curtains and turning off all the lights, I rumpled the bed and arranged the pillows, then made my way to the bathroom to change into my street clothes.

If my ruse failed, security was not just tight, it was triple-sealed. I was counting on human laziness and boredom: if I acted as expected and seemed anxious to follow all the rules, a cursory check would be deemed sufficient.

Walking through the glitzy lobby, I scanned the hotel bar and restaurant looking for someone who would be willing to help me. It was an intuitive process based on observation. The ideal candidate would speak English, value the bribe and be sympathetic to my cause.

I was looking for an individual but settled on a young couple that looked to be on a date, possibly their first, seated at a table far from the bar and the kitchen. The young woman was dressed for the occasion of a hotel dinner, the young man slightly less so, and he was studying the menu with the nervous attention of someone who couldn't afford the prices but couldn't appear too poor to afford the dinner intended to impress her. They exuded a charming awkwardness, and I decided to try them.

"Excuse me, but I'm hoping you speak English, May I ask you for help?"

Startled, they looked up at me, and I knew I would gain or lose their confidence in the first few seconds.

"If you could help me, I would be happy to treat you to dinner." To prove my good intentions, I slid large-denomination bills under his water glass, more than enough to buy full-course meals, wine and dessert, and enough left over for whatever else they might want to do that night. In doing so, I also placed my hotel room key-card on the table so they could see I was a legitimate guest.

The young man appraised me with suspicion but willingness to listen, and the young woman—her smooth cheeks subtly flecked with glittery make-up—appeared less sympathetic until I explained my real purpose: I wanted to look up a female friend I met in the States. I showed them Christine's address and the photo of her in front of City Hall.

I explained I needed their help getting to her flat, and in case she was out, introducing me to her mother. Of course I had no idea if she lived with her mother or if she was even at this address, but I needed to make it as easy as possible for them to say yes.

"You would be doing us a big favor," A little filial piety sweetens any pitch, so I said. "My flight was late and she has to stay with her mother. It's not very far away, is it?" I already knew it was a short drive—I'd selected this hotel from the limited options because it was the closest to her flat-- but reckoned ignorance might help my plea.

Though I couldn't understand their discussion, the young man appeared to champion my cause to win the sympathy of his date. It was a lot of money, and he could now afford to treat her to something special. He did not want to give that up, but did not want to look too desperate.

Sensing that she needed one more push to agree, I took the folded note inviting me to The Black Cat club. It seemed like years ago rather than a few short months.

"This is the note inviting me for our first date," I confided. "It's precious to me."

The young woman's eyes widened and it seemed she was impressed that Christine had invited me. The note added the veracity and romance I'd hoped for, and the young woman gathered up her purse and phone.

The young man ordered a taxi on his phone and we set off, me next to the driver and the couple in the back seat. The evening traffic was thankfully light. It was a peculiar setting for us all, strangers on a mission, and I broke the heavy silence by telling them about Christine attending our university, and the difficulties of getting an independent traveler visa.

The prospect of Christine answering the door heightened the tension, as I anticipated her shock and disapproval. I hoped to get past both. The prospect of it not being her address was also troubling, for that meant she had a complicated life here, too.

What I wanted was for her to open the door and embrace me with irrepressible happiness. Even though I knew that was a foolish fantasy, it was still what I wanted.

The address was a substantial townhouse in a neighborhood that predated all the recent booms and busts. Anyone who could afford to live here was more than well-off.

The young man accompanied me to the door. There were no lights, and I wondered if it was empty. I rang the bell twice, and eventually a light came on. The voice of an older woman crackled in the security panel and the young man responded. The woman's explanation was brief and the young man's expression fell. "This is the housemaid. She says the mother is in the hospital. She heard she passed away. She hasn't seen Christine in a long time."

Even in the dim light I must have looked ashen, for the young man murmured, "Sorry."

"Something bad has happened," I replied. I hoped for Christine's sake her Mom hadn't died, but the empty house was not a hopeful sign. At least I now knew this was still the family house, but none of them lived here.

We returned to the taxi and the couple conversed in low tones all the way back to the hotel.

I paid the driver and we entered the lobby. They hesitated, and the young man said apologetically, "We will have dinner somewhere else."

I said, "You have been very kind to me, thank you. You are good together. Please be happy together." They exchanged glances like young couples do on an eventful first date, and returned to the curb to catch another taxi.

I went to my room and collapsed on the bed. My mind was as disjointed as my sense of time. I must have fallen asleep, for I dreamed I was outside a neglected single-story house with tall weeds in the front yard, and suddenly I saw Christine in the window waving wanly to me. She was alone and forlorn.

*   *   *

My next step was to investigate the building that seemed the likely location of the camera. Since I'd moved the cathedral to the top of my list prior to my arrival, Mr. Hundred-Percent, again wearing a wide silk tie, this one of blue and gold, accompanied me without comment. Churches and architecture did not seem to be high on his list of interests, and so he sat on a shaded bench in the plaza looking at his phone while I joined a guided tour for visitors.

Before leaving him, I explained that I needed to circle the plaza after the guided tour to see the cathedral from all angles. He didn't even bother acknowledging my statement, and I realized that rather than lose the interpreter crapshoot, I'd won the jackpot. Mr. Hundred-

Percent appeared to disdain this assignment as beneath his ability and dignity, and was thus predisposed to dismiss me as an obsequious fool.

Occupied with plotting my next moves, I heard little of what the female guide said, and was grateful to blend in with a group of Westerners from a packaged tour. In case my phone camera was also monitored—and why wouldn't it be? —I snapped photos of whatever features were of obvious interest.

The tour ended, and I took a moment before leaving to visit one of the chapel altars to kneel and offer a sincere prayer for Heavenly guidance and assistance. The candle-lit altar, imbued with the prayers of generations of worshipers, filled the chapel space with a sense of tranquility and grace.

As I mentioned at the start, I lack the disposition for real faith. But this doesn't mean I lack the desire for grace. This brief prayer gave me solace: I had done all I could, and would accept the Will of God as manifested in fate or destiny.

Once outside, I texted Mr. Hundred-Percent that was circling the plaza, and proceeded to take dozens of photos to mask my interest in the four-story building. The double windows on each of the top three floors matched those in the video, and so I was sure this was the camera site.

Simple in design and quickly thrown together, it was outdated and poorly maintained, with visible rust streaks marring the flat white plaster facade. Devoid of decoration, it looked like a first-wave-of-modernization structure of the sort that were now being torn down and replaced with gleaming office towers. A narrow courtyard with a walkway and a few tired shrubs for landscaping separated the building from the sidewalk.

The building appeared to be office suites—small brass nameplates were affixed to the wall beside the glass entry doors—but a suite could be used for other purposes. I tried the door; it was locked.

To see the backside, I walked down the street behind the buildings facing the plaza. A small parking area occupied the rear of my target building. Threading my way through the parked cars, I checked the back entrance. It was also locked. The high percentage of luxury cars in the lot was at odds with the rather shabby state of the building; tenants wealthy enough to own these cars could afford nicer offices.

In the corner of the lot, a dumpster overflowing with white and black trash bags awaited emptying. Broken furniture and other rubbish had been left behind the dumpster.

I was at a dead end, and out of ideas on how to find someone who knew the building's occupants and could let me in who also happened to speak English. The incredible foolishness of this misadventure struck me hard, for this was always how it would end: no leads, no hope. It had always been impossible to find Christine, and now I was experiencing the impossibility firsthand.

Disgusted with myself, I trudged down the street in a state of ruin. An altercation down a small side street attracted my attention and I walked across the street for a closer look. Five rough-and-tumble young males in jeans and T-shirts were restraining a well-dressed young man in a white shirt and tie and his smartly-dressed winsome female companion. While two held the young man's arms, a third playfully pulled the young woman's purse. While she was occupied with this tug-of-war, the other two miscreants lifted her frilly knee-length skirt to expose her pink lace underwear and shapely derriere, to the guffaws of their fellows. Her shrill protests and attempts to punch the purse thief added to their enjoyment, and after a few more catcalls, they released the pair, who walked away muttering angrily and likely impotently, Glancing round to make sure the hoodlums weren't following, they hurried down the main street to a busier section.

Either the toughs had figured out this was a security camera blind spot where they could avoid official notice, or they were already outcasts and as long as they didn't do anything overly criminal, the authorities wouldn't bother intervening.

The normal person would naturally give the young toughs with time on their hands a wide berth, but these were just sort of lay-abouts who had time to watch the comings and goings of people who owned luxury cars, and who would be far more likely to know low-level employees such as maintenance and cleaning crews.

It's wise to have some slight edge when confronting a new risk, and I returned to the dumpster in the parking lot to retrieve a length of bamboo I'd spotted in the pile of broken furniture. A half-dozen pieces about four feet long were attached to a delaminating wood frame. Maybe it had been part of a decorative screen; the clear sealer had peeled off, leaving the bamboo partially weathered by exposure to the elements. Once length came loose with the first tug and I used it as a walking stick.

I might be able to distract two toughs long enough to escape, but five were way too many to deal with. The problem with any weapon is it can be wrested away and used against you, so the first goal is to keep it away from the hands of opponents. Still, I felt more confident having a familiar weapon in my hand rather than nothing.

Pausing, at the entrance to the side street, I texted Mr. Hundred-Percent that I was thirsty and was going to buy a drink.

The alley was lined with typical storefront bays, each secured by a rolldown metal door that sealed the entire bay. Most of the doors were down. I walked to the open bay where one lean tough was outside smoking a cigarette. It was a café with a few tables and a counter with canned and bottled drinks and the tools to make fresh tea and coffee. Bright advertising banners and posters covered the walls, and strings of cheap red paper lanterns had been strung between the ceiling lights.

A somewhat older man in khaki trousers and a tropical-hued shirt held court on the largest table, surrounded by the younger toughs who'd amused themselves harassing the bourgeois couple. I pointed to a bottle of water and as I was paying, asked the young man behind the counter if anyone spoke English, Peering at me through heavy-framed glasses, he nodded, and I motioned him to follow me to the leader's table.

The leader sported a neatly trimmed moustache and a pair of expensive sunglasses hung off his shirt pocket. He looked at me with the interest one pays to a welcome distraction from boredom.

"You have drugs?" he asked.

"No, sorry, Boss," I replied. "Something else." I took out the photo of Christine and placed it on the table in front of him. "She's in that white building down the street." I glanced at the youth with the glasses and pointed to his boss. He took the cue and translated my pitch.

"I want to know which suite she goes to, and I need a key to get in."

The boss glanced at the photo and made a dismissive comment.

My interpreter said, "He said she's okay but he can get you a much prettier girl."

"I thank you kindly," I said to the boss, and half-bowed politely. "But I want this girl and will pay for the key."

The boss gazed at me and muttered something which the interpreter did not translate, and I caught the drift. "I don't have the money on me. I will bring it when you locate the girl and the key." My interpreter translated my statement and the boss chuckled, and what he said was summarized by the interpreter. "He said why should we bother helping you?"

I'd already thought through a plan if I found someone who might be able to get me information on Christine. I laid out my offer: the cash equivalent of a year's pay for a white-collar manager for the boss, 50% of that for whomever brought the information and key to him, 25% to whomever had helped the second fellow, 12.5% to the next link in the chain and so on. Even the fourth and fifth links would get a useful chunk of cash for digging around.

I didn't know the formal name of this incentive system, but I knew it worked wonders on unearthing information fast.

The boss's skeptical comment was duly translated. "How do I know you have that much money?"

I'd changed money in the airport and I showed him the conversion receipt. That evidence impressed him and he considered my offer with visibly heightened interest. In his shoes, I would be thinking about saying he had the key when he didn't, and then robbing me when I showed up.

I then played my ace. "I have an official interpreter," I said. "He's ex-military and hates difficulties. He's outside waiting for me. He knows right where I am. His boss also hates difficulties."

This set the boss back a bit, and he chuckled again. His joke prompted uneasy laughter.

"I need the key by Sunday morning, or the offer expires," I said. "I need a key to the building, and a key or entry code to the girl's suite."

The boss mulled the conditions and made a comment. My interpreter said, "He asks why this girl is worth so much money."

Reckoning it was better to drop a hint that left the spaces blank, I replied, "We met in America. That's all I can tell you."

I then issued my instructions. "My phone is monitored, so send me this message when you have the keys: 'I have the information about the church bells for you.' Then send a man on a motorbike to my hotel. Have him bring a spare helmet for me."

The boss nodded, and I glanced around at his squad. They had lost their languid boredom and were shifting restlessly in the folding chairs.

I stood up and bowed respectfully to the boss. "I hope we can do business together."

He gave me a wry look and nodded.

*   *   *

I'd readied a plan for incentivizing locals to unearth information about Christine, but not for what I would do if we met. There were two considerations: what I wanted, and what was possible given her unspecified constraints. She'd made it clear that coming back to the States was not possible. But what about marrying me in private here? Or arranging for me to get a work permit so we could see each other? I concluded the only thing that really mattered was her telling me the truth. But would she?

I anticipated her shock at my intrusion and anger at me ignoring her wishes to not follow her. Though I hoped for a reconciliation and some happier resolution, I was resigned to the possibility that all I would get was her anger. She protected herself very carefully, and my upsetting those plans would not make her happy. My viewing the wretched sex party video would also not please her. No one wants their humiliation to be broadcast, and whatever she was hiding had been partially revealed in the video: the functionaries had something unbreakable on her.

But all that lay in the future. I was hopeful the Alley Gang would find a way to bribe a maintenance worker to duplicate the keys, but that was very much in doubt. The odds favored a dead end and me never locating Christine, much less getting to meet her. Maybe the gang would rat me out to score some points with the local authorities and I'd be deported tomorrow. There were many paths to failure and only one to success.

My job was to spend Saturday lulling Mr. Hundred-Percent with more evidence I was an obsequious fool. My itinerary took us to an impressive Buddhist temple that had been rebuilt after a fire in the late 1700s and again in the early 1900s. Mr. Hundred-Percent wore a red silk tie with yellow dots, and again found a comfortable place to look at his phone while I went through the motions of being interested in the massive tree-trunk posts, ornate carvings and rich symbolism of the decorations. I repeated the pattern of strolling around the neighborhood and texting him that I was buying a drink.

It was an uneventful day and we were both relieved to end it early. Sunday was his day off, and if I wanted to leave the hotel I would need to arrange another officially approved interpreter beforehand. I told Mr. Hundred-Percent that I was jetlagged and needed to take Sunday off. His lack of acknowledgement was encouraging, for the less interest he had in me, the better.

I awoke early Sunday and set about staging a day apparently spent in my hotel room. Taking the elevator to the lobby, I asked the front desk to please arrange maid service at the earliest possible time as I would be in my room for the day.

I then had a leisurely breakfast in the hotel restaurant—congee, noodles, pickles and other local favorites—and returned to my room as the stout maid was finishing up. I gave her a generous tip and smiled my thanks as she bowed politely and left.

I'd decided to make my way to Christine's building even if I heard nothing from the Alley Gang, on the faint hope that I might find one of the entry doors open or happen upon someone entering or leaving. Once inside, I would wander around the third and fourth floors, hoping for some evidence or clue. It was a threadbare plan doomed to fail, but I couldn't pace the hotel room berating myself all day.

The problem was how to get there without hiring a taxi, as any monitored means of travel was not allowed without a guide. I would have to leave my phone on the nightstand to avoid being tracked, but this deprived me of the means to get messages from the Alley Gang.

While I was pondering these tradeoffs, my phone chirped and with hands palsied by anticipation I opened the message: "information on church bells available." It was the miracle I'd prayed for at the chapel altar. I texted a reply "okay thanks" and hurriedly stuffed hotel envelopes with the appropriate sums of cash, plus five for the gang, each with enough to fund an evening's dining and entertainment.

Reminding myself not to appear nervous or hurried, I went down to the lobby and found a chair from which I could watch the stretch of canopied pavement outside the entry for a motorbike. Minutes passed like hours but I knew the distance and could estimate the travel time, as traffic was light on Sunday morning.

A motorbike did a U-turn and stopped behind a taxi. A uniformed bellhop gestured the motorbike driver to move, but the driver ignored him and raced the engine. Unable to restrain myself, I ran out and peered into the helmet visor. The driver nodded and handed me a helmet. I barely slipped it over my head when he roared off, nearly pitching me into the pavement.

His high-speed maneuvers raised the possibility that I might be killed on the street just as success was in reach, but we screeched to halt in the alley. Pulling off the helmet, I went in and found the gang at the bar drinking tea. Wary of being cheated, I greeted the boss and said, "There are six of you and one of me. Would you please show me the keys or codes first?"

The boss placed an old-fashioned entry key on the table and an index card with the numbers 43—the suite number--and 4447, the entry code. I took out the packets of incentive cash, each labeled in descending order: Boss, 2, 3,4, 5 and 6, and with a slight bow passed them to the boss. He slowly counted the cash in each envelope and then nodded his approval. First asking for his permission via my interpreter, I handed out the lesser packets to each gang member as a gesture of appreciation.

The boss's expression tightened and he made a brief comment. I'd anticipated a further squeeze and so was not surprised when my interpreter said, "He said there were expenses." Shrugging, I handed the boss my wallet. I'd left enough to be useful but no more. He looked slightly disappointed but took the bills and then handed me the wallet.

He motioned for me to show him my passport holder around my neck, and I did so reluctantly. But that was for show, as it had neither my passport or cash, only hotel receipts, as I'd stashed my plastic-bagged passport, visa and cash in my shoes.

Satisfied he'd stripped the goose of all its feathers, he gave me a gruff send-off, which was duly translated as, "I hope she's worth it."

I left before the boss had any further ideas and walked rapidly up the street to the building's dumpster and pried off another length of bamboo. This prepared me to deal with the possibility of persuading the functionaries to let Christine leave with me.

Proceeding to the back entrance of the building, with great satisfaction I clicked the lock open and entered. Taking the stairs two at a time, I reached the fourth floor and paused to catch my breath. My heart continued racing, for this was the moment I'd been anticipating, Would Christine be here, or would the suite be empty? Or would there be another sex party, but no Christine? I reached Suite 43 and heard no sounds inside. Readying myself for whatever I might find, I punched in the entry code and opened the door.

Christine was standing by the first bed, tugging a stunning white strapless wedding dress up over her bosom. The high-waisted dress reached her ankles in wavelets of crenelated white lace. It looked as lavish as anything in the Versailles of Louis the Sixteenth.

She froze at the sight of me, too shocked to utter a word.

Behind her, a straight-backed wooden chair awaited. The intended use was evidenced by a homemade cat-o-nine-tails of multiple strands of knotted cord draped on the back of the chair.

Behind the chair stood one of the men from the dismal sex party. He wore a pair of blue boxer shorts and was in the act of adjusting a video camera on a tripod to capture his misuse of the faux bride-to-be.

While the scene appeared to be costumed sex-play featuring entertainment courtesy of the bride, Christine's wedding gown made me realize this man probably had the power to force marriage on her, something even worse than the more blatant bondage he already imposed on her.

The thought that she might have already been forced into marrying him boiled my blood, and in reaction to my visible rage he backed toward a canvas bag on a low table by the window. He was either reaching for a phone to call for help or a weapon, and since I couldn't allow him access to either, I dropped the bamboo stick and sprinted toward him, landing a flying side-kick on his breastbone.

As the Professor had so ably described, there are moments when the Tao flows and everything is perfect: the football spirals perfectly to the leaping receiver, the basketball launched from three-point range swishes through the net, or in this case, a flying kick, concentrating the entire energy of my accelerating leap on a few square inches of the opponent's center of gravity.

Given my size, speed, training and rage, the man flew backwards against the aluminum window mullion, which gave way as easily as a thin stick of balsa wood. The man, mullion and the two panes of glass disappeared from view as gravity took them to earth. The crash of glass marked their impact.

With the breeze blowing against my damp skin, I approached the gaping hole and leaned over the remaining wall to look below. The man had fallen directly on two unfortunates standing on the walkway below the window, snapping their necks like twigs. The window glass had mopped up any remaining life in the three men.

Christine joined me in peering down at the carnage. In a voice of disbelief, she said, "You killed them all."

In shock, I said, "I intended to hurt him, not kill him."

Stepping back from the window, in a trembling voice, she said, "You've ruined everything."

"No, he ruined everything," I replied. "Did he force you to marry him?"

Her response was to burst into tears. Beside herself, she sobbed, "You don't know what you've done. You've ruined everything." Overcome, she fell to her knees and wept with such anguish that I could not imagine what could break her reserve so completely. She wept without restraint for painfully long moments, and I realized it was everything she'd endured and everything she'd kept locked up inside her pouring forth in an uncontrolled flood. She was mourning all she'd sacrificed and lost, and I could not imagine the enormity of that.

The flood subsided as the dam drained. Recovering, but still kneeling, she said, "You don't understand. You've ruined everything."

"I'm sorry, but destiny had other plans."

She looked at me with tear-stained resentment. "No one made you come here. Destiny had nothing to do with it."

"Okay, but what do we do now?"

The shattered Christine reverted to the Christine I knew. Standing up, she ordered, "Help me out of this stupid dress." I unzipped the back and tugged it to the floor. She wore no underwear and I saw the inflamed lines of her tormenter's morning pleasure on her derriere.

"We have to hurry," she said. "They'll be up here any minute." A closet and bathroom occupied the corner I didn't see in the video, and she went to the closet and hastily pulled on jeans and a pullover top, instructing, "Get his bag, the memory in the camera and your bamboo stick. You didn't touch anything else, did you?"

"Just the entry keypad and the door handle." Retrieving a washcloth from the bathroom, she said, "Wipe the camera after you get the memory chip and the door handle when we leave." After pulling the memory from the camera, I wiped it clean. Snatching her purse from the first bed, we left and I wiped the handle and keypad as instructed. "What about security cameras?" I asked.

"Didn't you notice? There aren't any. This building is their private getaway."

Hurrying down the stairs, we paused by the rear exit and she reached into the dead man's canvas bag and pulled out car keys. "Even when they realize he's dead, they won't be surprised that I'm taking his car to his private flat. I often drove his car there," she explained. "We need to find something there."

Clicking the key fob, the locks on a midnight-blue luxury car opened and she slid behind the steering wheel. "Lay down on the back seat," she instructed. "If I'm alone, that's not going to raise alarms."

"How far is it?" I asked.

"Pretty far. We'll only have a few minutes to find the database before they send somebody to his flat to do their own search. It's probably on a memory stick."

"What database?"

"The man you killed compiled a secret database of all the party and government bigshots' accounts and assets in the West. It was his ultimate protection against rivals, and his ultimate source of influence. We need to find it."

"What's the plan once we find it?"

"Get to the river and get on a barge carrying bricks or something upriver and disappear."

That sounded dubious to me, but at this point it was one step at a time.

Doubled up on the backseat, I couldn't see her. "You said, 'you killed them all.' Who's all?"

"The Gang of Three," she replied. "Mr. N. and his two top cronies."

"You mean his two top guys happened to be standing beneath the window at that moment?"

"Uh-huh. What timing. They were probably having a cigarette before coming up and joining the fun."

"Were they at the parties?"

She was silent for a long moment. "So you know about those. Yes, they were there. It was their idea of Sunday fun."

"Did Mr. N. force you to marry him?"

She snorted derisively. "No, he's already married. I was just one of his playthings."

Before I could ask my next question, she had one of her own. "How did you find me and get the key code? Who helped you?"

"It's a long story," I said. "Nobody helped me. I helped myself."

She absorbed this and I said, "Since we have a few minutes, could you please tell me what I ruined and what's going on?"

"I don't know," she said brusquely.

"I visited your house and met your housemaid," I said. "She said your Mom died. I'm sorry, if that's true."

Christine was quiet and then sighed. "Yes, it's true. Her heart was broken, and that broke the rest of her."

"I'm sorry," I repeated, and she asked, "How did you get the address of my family home?"

"Subterfuge," I replied.

"I'm impressed," she murmured. "Did you really want to find me that badly?"

"It's all I've been living for," I replied. "But what did I ruin? And before you say 'I don't know,' don't I have a right to know?"

She was silent long enough that I reckoned she'd clammed up for good.

"I'm pregnant," she announced. "With our baby. Yours and mine."

Now I was the one shocked into silence. "And what did that ruin?"

"Nothing," she replied. "It's wonderful."

"That's a relief," I said. "I think it's wonderful, too. Couldn't you have told me?"

"Here's the problem," she said. "It only makes sense if you understand the Asian family and Asian politics."

"Well, educate me," I said. "I don't claim to understand Asian culture, but I might be less dunderheaded than you imagine."

"It's upsetting," she said. "You won't like it."

"I don't have to like it; I just have to hear the truth. Then I'll understand."

She sighed again and said, "Political families run things in Asia. Not necessarily blood ties families, but ties close enough to be family, from schools, neighborhoods, first jobs in the bureaucracy, military service, connections to old families that are political royalty, all that."

"Okay."

"My father was a bigshot in a political clan that was on the rise. To use your word, he was destined for high positions in the government and party. He got rich from the business connections that come with the job, and he bought us that house and a vacation home in the mountains. My Mom was happy to be rich and influential. She reveled in my father's rise."

"Those make everybody happy."

"Yes, but they're built on sand. Political winds shift."

She was quiet again. "I really don't know how to say this politely, so I'll just say it. My father had mistresses, like all bigshots. One was the daughter of a bigshot in a rival family. Her Western name is Missy."

"So her father didn't like that."

"it was more complicated than that," she said. "Her father is Mr. N. Missy had designs on an alliance of the two political families, an alliance that would make each more powerful. This would help her father and make her a player."

"So she agreed to be your father's mistress as part of a power-politics plan."

"Yes," Christine confirmed. "Sex, money and politics always go together. The problem is my father lied to Missy. Maybe he actually believed he was infertile, but in any event, that's what he told her, but he wasn't, and so Missy got pregnant."

"That's not uncommon," I said. "The mistress ends the pregnancy and life goes on."

"Except she kept the baby, a girl," Christine replied. "But she kept it a secret, She got a visa to the States and only sent her parents photos of her face, not her belly, so when she gave birth to my father's baby, her parents were shocked."

"I can imagine."

"Out of wedlock babies are still frowned on here," Christine explained. "It makes a good marriage impossible. Missy and my father tried to arrange a wedding to a young guy before the baby was born but her parents found out and demanded DNA tests."

"It's getting messy," I commented.

"It's about to get even messier," Christine said, and I had the feeling that this unburdening was a relief to her.

"Missy's parents were furious with her for having the baby and furious at my father for not being careful with their daughter. An affair is okay if it's mutual, and this one made sense politically. Missy could have had this fling and then married well in her late 20s. But now she has a baby who everyone knows was fathered by my Dad."

"So then what?"

"All this might have blown over, but my Dad's clan lost power while Mr. N.'s rose to the top. It's too complicated to explain, but my father was disgraced and had to resign. This meant Missy's father now had the upper hand and could get revenge."

"But how?"

"I can't believe I'm telling you this," Christine said flatly. "It's something I vowed never to tell you."

"I'm glad you trust me."

"It's not trust, it's fear," she said. "I'm afraid of what you'll think."

"Well, let's just assume I think nothing."

"No, you'll think something," she warned. "Something bad."

"I'd rather have an ugly truth than a pretty lie."

"This is the ugly truth," she said. "Missy's father had my Dad thrown in prison on corruption charges. That's what happens when you lose power or are disgraced. Mr. N. made it clear that the only way my father could ever get out of prison is if I let Missy's father make me pregnant and I have his baby, just like Missy had my father's."

"Tit for tat," I said hollowly. "But wait, Missy's child is your half-sister."

"Yes, and if I'd agreed to have Mr. N.'s baby, the baby would have been Missy's half brother or sister."

"But you didn't agree."

"Yes, I did," she corrected me. "I couldn't let my father stay in prison for the rest of his life, and watch my mother waste away from the disgrace. This is what you won't understand: I had no choice but to agree. Regardless of my own feelings, I had to agree."

"Okay, you agreed, but worked out a way around it."

"Yes. I demanded three things. I demanded a semester in the States as my last bit of freedom before I became his mistress and a mom, and no cameras or bugs in my American flat. I refused to be watched like an inmate in a prison cell. The third demand was as soon as I was pregnant, my father would be freed."

"I know about your two flats," I interjected. "That was very clever, cutting a passageway in the closets."

"You're better than I expected," she said. "I knew they'd bug my flat anyway, but less obtrusively, so I could crawl along the floor and slip into my second flat, the one where we met."

"So the idea was to secretly get pregnant in the States, then go back right away and claim Missy's father had made you pregnant. But why, and why me?"

"Put yourself in my shoes," she replied. "What sweet revenge to have Mr. N. in the delivery room, watching his revenge-baby being born with such joy, and seeing a half-Western baby pop out."

"But what about your father? Wouldn't he have been arrested?"

"I got him and my Mom exit visas to the West once I was pregnant and he was freed," she explained. "If my Mom hadn't been so ill, she would have joined my Dad. But he's in the West now, laying low. They can't punish him anymore. And they can't punish my Mom any more, either."

I broke the silence by repeating my question. "Why me?"

She chuckled mordantly. "At first, it was just genes," she explained. "Of course I wanted handsome, smart genes but just as important, genes with integrity and a rebellious streak."

"I'm honored."

"Of course I had to be physically and emotionally attracted to the father," she said. "Getting pregnant is a lot easier if you're in love, and so I wanted to fall in love."

"So that's why you were wondering if you were really in love with me, or had just convinced yourself that you were in love."

"Yes. But I knew as soon as our hands touched in The Black Cat I was drawn to you."

"And you were under time pressure," I said, "so voila."

"Yes, voila."

"I think there's another word for it: seduction."

"Ooh, I like the sound of that," she purred. "I seduced you."

"Yes, and you were very good at it."

In a tone of self-mockery, she said, "A girl does what's needed."

"And you needed, um, voila."

"Yes. But I have something else to tell you. This is my second pregnancy. My first boyfriend and I hatched a wild plan for me to get pregnant and we'd run away to the West, living in sin so our families would renounce us. Then we'd have been free of all the family burdens."

"What happened?"

"It took longer than expected to get pregnant, I had a miscarriage, and he gave up our dream to become a boring functionary like everyone else."

"Are you worried about losing this baby?"

"Of course, but everything feels right this time. It felt right from the start."

I was nonplussed, and she continued. "You know when we made love in that spot on the cliffs? Afterward I had this feeling, I can't describe it, an awareness that I was pregnant. I'd never heard anyone else having that feeling right after making love, so I wanted to dismiss it but couldn't."

"You kept saying something had changed in you."

"Yes, but I couldn't tell you I was pregnant."

"I felt the change in you," I said. "I just didn't know the reason why."

"My history of miscarriage turned out to be very useful," she continued. "I bribed a doctor to say that sex would cause another miscarriage due to my delicate condition, and so I wasn't forced to do it with Mr. N. or anyone else after the few times needed to make him believe he'd made me pregnant."

In a sarcastic, tittering tone she added, "He was so proud of his virility. It became part of his personal legend that 'he only had to bang her twice to make a baby.' What a loss of face once everyone knew the baby wasn't his."

"So he and his buddies took revenge in other ways," I commented, and she murmured, "I can't believe they're dead, and I won't get my revenge. It was all I had to keep me going."

"That loss of face might have triggered even worse things," I said.

"We're getting close to the flat now," she reported, and her voice tightened with a renewed anxiety.

"One last thing," I said. "Will you marry me?"

Her tone expressed incredulity. "After all that, the first thing you say is you want to marry me?"

"Of course. You made every sacrifice uncomplainingly. You played a terrible hand brilliantly, and saved her father. You're a heroine to me and I want to marry you right here in the backseat."

"We'll have to put it off a bit," she said, and then pulled the car into a stall behind a two-story house. "Don't look hurried. You take his bag."

I followed her up the stairs and into the flat. She closed the door behind us and disabled the security system with a code. It was modernist, with floor to ceiling windows and wood blinds, and Scandinavian furniture mixed with Asian accents and a mix of Asian and Western art. It looked lightly lived in.

"Did he live here?"

"No, this is his private flat," she answered. "I came here a few times with him. This is where he brought his other mistresses. I got the dreary room with lumpy mattresses and the others got this."

Glancing around, she said, "I'm not sure where to even start looking. I'm sure he was careful."

"Everyone gets ideas from movies," I commented. "We should open picture frames, check the bottom of vases, and look for anything out of place in chandeliers."

"No chandeliers here," she said. "He wouldn't leave it someplace obvious. It's too important."

"What kind of guy was he?" I asked. "What was his college degree?"

"Engineering," she replied.

"What kind? Electrical?"

"Maybe," she said. "I'm not sure."

"We should take the covers off all the light switches and outlets," I suggested. "They're the perfect hiding place for a memory stick and nobody thinks of them, except maybe an engineer or builder."

"How did you think of it?"

"It's where I would hide it," I said. "The base of floor and desk lamps are also good hiding places. I need a screwdriver. Do bigshots have a tool drawer?"

"No, but their employees do. His assistants would come by when he wasn't with a mistress." As she rummaged through a drawer in the kitchen she murmured. "I wish I knew how much time we have. We don't want to be trapped here."

She found a multi-tip screwdriver and handed it to me.

"Well then, we better find it fast. I'll check all the electrical places, you check the undersides of desks, chairs, bookcases, vases, look for false bottoms in desk drawers, and look behind every painting and under every art piece."

As we worked, I said, "Could you start a rumor he committed suicide? That might be useful."

"That's probably what the official investigation will conclude. It's clean and easy, and everyone knew about his database, so his death will be seen as a great blessing by everyone but his family. And who knows, maybe even them. He was still estranged from Missy."

We'd only been working a few minutes when voices approached the front door. Waving me into the hallway, Christine rushed to the canvas bag and pulled out a small-caliber pistol. That surprised me, as guns were restricted. But cautious Mr. N. must have acquired one just in case.

Clicking off the safety, she ran into the kitchen as the front door opened and two young men in slacks, white shirts and ties entered with the casualness of familiarity.

They did not seemed alarmed, and so they couldn't have known about the death of their boss. One went to the refrigerator to scrounge a beverage, and he soon entered the living room, sans beverage, with Christine's gun in his back. His pal was dumbstruck by the girl with the gun, and in a harsh voice she ordered them to lay on the floor and put their hands behind their backs.

"Get the duct tape out of the kitchen drawer and tape up their hands and ankles," she told me. Once I'd bound them as instructed, she searched their pockets and took their phones, wallets and car keys. "Drag them into the bedroom closet," she said. "Then we'll cover their mouths and tape them back-to-back."

"If they don't know where the database is, I'll kill them," she said. Their squirming in terror indicated they understood English, and she winked at me. In the same harsh tone of authority, she demanded they share the whereabouts of the memory stick. Of course nothing that important would be revealed to underlings, but I guessed that Christine was hoping they might have some clues. They babbled responses which even I could tell were denials.

"Ask them if their boss was an electrical engineer," I suggested. She did so, one answered, and she nodded confirmation.

I dragged the unlucky employees to the walk-in closet and taped them up as instructed while Christine held the gun on them. It looked awfully comfortable in her hand, and once we closed the closet door, I murmured, "You look like you know what you're doing with that."

"I was in what you call ROTC," she said.

"Did they say anything useful?"

Shaking her head, she said, "No. It was just a rumor as far as they knew."

Confident an electrical engineer would choose a hiding place within the electrical system, I suggested Christine check lamps and light fixtures while I checked switches and outlets.

"I can't reach those lights," she said, pointing to the indirect cove lighting hidden behind wood crown molding that ran along the top of the living room walls. That seemed like a good hiding place to me, and so I dragged a dining chair to the perimeter of the room, moving furniture so I could reach into the trough to feel for anything taped to the inside.

It was a daunting task, and I interrupted Christine to ask, "What would he use to mark where he hid the memory stick up here? What about one of these paintings or photos? Were any significant to him?"

She scanned the art and pointed to an arty black-and-white photo of a reclining young woman's bare thighs, derriere and dimpled small of her back. The shadow cast by the photographer slanted across the well-lit warmth of the woman's body. It had the intimacy of a self-portrait.

I imagined Mr. N,'s perverse pleasure with Christine's every flinch under his blows, and now he was but a shadow. The photo seemed a foretelling of his fate.

Positioning the chair in front of the photo, I searched the inner surfaces of the cove boards. I was about to give up when I ran my finger along the top edge of the back board and felt a lump. Carefully prying it loose, I looked at what was under the tape: a memory stick.

"I think I found it," I announced. If this wasn't the database, why had he gone to such pains to hide it? Pushing it deep into her pocket, she said, "Okay, let's go."

Going to his desk, she took a piece of paper and scribbled a note in her native language. "This says he committed suicide," she explained, "and that I followed him. I'm leaving my phone here. Never turn your phone off or smash the card, that's a red flag."

Spotting a pair of designer sunglasses in the desk clutter, she handed the shades to me and said, "We won't fool facial recognition, but it doesn't hurt to try." Taking two broad-brimmed hats off a shelf, she handed one to me and piled her hair beneath the other one. Putting on her own sunglasses and placing the two employee's phones in her purse, she said, "I'd cut my hair to throw them off but we don't have time. Let's go."

As we trotted down the steps to the sidewalk, I asked, "How will we get to the river?"

"We hire motorcycles at the street market. It's only two blocks away."

The street had been closed to make a pedestrian-only market of temporary stalls, and the vendors were busy on this sunny Sunday. Pausing by a noodle vendor with two tiny tables for customers, Christine set Mr. N.'s employees' phones on the table, studied the menu, and then walked away, leaving the phones.

Motorcycles waiting for vendor deliveries clustered at one end of the street, and Christine spoke to two young drivers who had been chatting with each other. Opening her purse, she paid them and beckoned me.

After stuffing our hats in her purse, we pulled on the proffered helmets, climbed on the back of the two motorcycles and roared off toward the river. It was an exhilarating ride, not just due to the youthful drivers' hair-raising skills in weaving through traffic, but in the sense that we'd escaped—at least so far.

The motorcyclists left us on a weedy patch of cracked asphalt at the far end of a riverside quay, beyond the pole-mounted security cameras, and we gazed up and down the shore for a boat on which we could buy passage or stow away.

Christine's freight barges were churning along in the middle of river, and our prospects for a clean getaway dimmed considerably. Small water-taxis crossed the river at designated docks, and an occasional tourist boat drifted past, but there didn't seem to be any barges being loaded with cargo. The idea was to avoid docks with security cameras and find some obscure loading point. There didn't seem to be any.

At the end of the quay, a single-masted yacht was tied to the last dock cleat, and a Westerner was on deck, attending to the rigging. I suggested, "Let's go ask that guy."

Christine was skeptical. "I don't know. I'd rather find a local who will keep their mouth shut."

"There's no harm in asking," I replied, and as I approached the sailor she anxiously scanned the waters for an alternative.

The man was slight in build, a bit older than me, with sun-bleached, untrimmed hair and an air of self-containment. "Where you heading?" I asked.

"Not sure yet," he replied. "Maybe across the Pacific."

"Would you be willing to take two passengers?"

He glanced at me and Christine, who had stopped uncertainly a few yards away. It was a lonely spot, and not a place pleasure-seekers would visit. I read his understanding that we were in trouble in his eyes. "Have you got any money?"

"Yes," I replied. "Enough to make it worthwhile."

"How much is worthwhile?"

"Equal to first-class tickets on an airline," I offered.

"The cabin is small," he noted. "There won't be much privacy."

"That's not really a priority for us right now," I said.

"Well, what is?"

His gaze was sharp but not unfriendly, and with so little time and so much to lose, I said, "Getting away from security cameras would be a start."

"Trouble with the little lady?"

"I just sent her boss to the Other Side," I confessed. "It was an accident. He went out a fourth-floor window."

He seemed amused by this tragedy and the pickle I'd put us in.

"I take it you're in a bit of a hurry."

"You could say that."

"Why don't you show me your first-class fares and let's ask the little lady to inspect the accommodations."

Removing my shoes, I showed him my passport, visa, counted out the bulk of my cash and handed it to him.

He counted it himself and asked, "Anything else I should know?"

"She's pregnant. It's mine."

Scratching his head, he said, "That's quite a situation. Why don't you bring the little lady on board."

I motioned to Christine and she approached reluctantly. "He's crossing the Pacific. We can get out of here and not be traced. He wants you to look at the cabin."

"I don't know," she said, and I pressed her. "We're out of options. If we don't leave soon, they'll find us. They'll find the employees, figure out we dropped their phones at the market and then check the taxis and motorcyclists there."

With obvious reluctance she accompanied me onto the boat and glanced in the cabin. The captain said, "You two can bunk in the private bed up front."

"Can this boat cross the Pacific?" she asked.

"It's done it many times," he said, "with a port of call in Hawaii."

"It's so small," she observed, and he shrugged. "It's a yacht, not a super-yacht."

Returning to the quay, Christine looked at me, and I suddenly understood the source of her reluctance. It wasn't the boat or the captain; it was me.

She was accustomed to being on her own, answering to nothing but her own sense of duty and righteousness. The only way she could commit to anything, or anyone, is if she wasn't beholden. She needed me, I needed her, and our unborn child needed us both. And at this critical moment, we needed this captain and his boat, or we would soon be separated and imprisoned, with extremely dim prospects. But trying to force a commitment only alienated her. She would do anything to avoid being trapped, but we were trapped.

She wanted to be needed and appreciated, but not confined by that love. I understood this all at once, and the words came with the understanding.

"If we stay here," I said, "we'll be arrested, separated and imprisoned. I doubt we'll ever get out, at least not alive. Our baby will be born in prison and taken from you. They can't get your father, but they'll have you and the baby instead. If that's what you want, go ahead and stand there looking at barges pass by until the police arrive. But I'm going on this boat. I already paid passage for both of us. You owe me nothing, and I don't owe you anything, either. But don't we owe our child something better than prison? But you do whatever you want. I'm not forcing you, or even arguing with you. I'll go my way and you go yours."

I turned away, struck by the irony of it. She could only accept love if you first proved you wouldn't bind her, and the only way to do so was to reject her. Only then did she feel free.

The captain busied himself with casting off the bow lines, and Christine stepped on board. "At least we have the private bed," she said, and I embraced her. "It's a floating palace," I said, and the captain came aft to start the inboard engine and cast off the aft line.

We were free.

*　　*　　*

That's as far as I can take the story because the ending hasn't happened yet. Either we drown out here and no one will ever know what happened to us, or this little yacht holds together and our pirate-captain manages to sail it to the Hawaiian Islands. Most things fail, but I wouldn't discount our chances. The weather seems to be diminishing, the yacht has managed many a storm and our captain got us this far. And he's confident. I'm not sure why, but he's confident we'll make it. I'm confident, too, in my own way, because my prayers were answered and Christine's plan to make the database public by spreading it over thousands of servers and printed copies so it can never be erased has its own destiny.

Our pirate-captain has navigated the pitching cabin to bring me a bottle of water. I thank him and drink half, then lurch over to share the other half with Christine. She sits up, back against the cabin wall, and smiles at me. We have a future, and we both know it.

Finis

Made in the USA
Monee, IL
20 January 2024

52094630R00055